Damien Leith was born in Ireland and became an Australian citizen in January 2007. He is also an accomplished singer/songwriter and has released four albums through Sony Music Australia. Damien lives in Sydney with his wife and two sons. HarperCollins published Damien's first novel, *One More Time*, in 2007.

Visit Damien Leith's websites:
www.damienleith.com.au
www.myspace.com/damienleith

Also by Damien Leith

One More Time

DAMIEN LEITH

Remember June

HarperCollins*Publishers*

HarperCollins*Publishers*

First published in Australia in 2010
by HarperCollins*Publishers* Australia Pty Limited
ABN 36 009 913 517
harpercollins.com.au

HarperCollins*Publishers*
25 Ryde Road, Pymble, Sydney, NSW 2073, Australia
31 View Road, Glenfield, Auckland 0627, New Zealand
A 53, Sector 57, Noida, UP, India
77–85 Fulham Palace Road, London, W6 8JB, United Kingdom
2 Bloor Street East, 20th floor, Toronto, Ontario M4W 1A8, Canada
10 East 53rd Street, New York NY 10022, USA

National Library of Australia Cataloguing-in-Publication data:

Leith, Damien, 1976– .
  Remember June.
  ISBN: 978 0 7322 8682 8.
  I. Title.
A823.4

Cover design by Nada Backovic Designs
Cover image © amanaimages/Corbis
Author photo by Darren Leigh Roberts (dlrphoto.com.au)
Typeset in 11.5/18 Sabon by Kirby Jones

For Eileen, Jarvis, Jagger
and all my family near and far

Remember June

1984

'What's that, Daddy?' The child watched his father in awe.

'It's hair gel, Mattie, it's for styling your hair.'

'Styling?'

'Yea, it makes you look a bit slicker!'

'Can I have some?'

Dave smiled gently at his three-year-old son. How astoundingly quickly he was growing up. What had happened to the days when Dave could comfortably rest Mattie's entire body along his arm and watch his baby boy as he slept?

'I suppose we could put a little bit through your hair — but for heaven's sake, say nothing to your mother. The last thing she'll be wanting is to see you with your hair pasted to your skull. Let's make it our wee secret!'

Mattie threw Dave a mischievous grin. He didn't

always understand everything his father said but he knew that there was something secretive about what they were doing.

Rubbing a fingernail's length of Brylcreem between the palms of his hands, Dave reached out to his son and smoothed the cream through his hair. The boy's jet-black strands were much thicker than his father's, and curled at the ends. Dave always said that a good, strong head of hair was the key to any handsome man, and often used himself as an example. He had no doubt that Mattie was growing up to have the same gifts and would certainly be popular with the ladies.

'There now, you look fantastic.'

'I can't see, Daddy, can you lift me up?' Mattie bobbed up and down trying to catch a glimpse of himself in the mirror. 'Help me, Daddy!'

'All right, don't get your knickers in a twist!' Dave laughed and grappled a hold of his son and raised him. 'There you are now, you're almost as handsome-looking as your old man!'

Stephen
&
June

Stonebridge was a small but charming town, an hour south of Dublin. Its two major streets ran parallel to one another, beginning at the bridge from which the town got its name, where the Catholic parish church held a commanding stance, and stretching down to the Protestant church about half a mile away. In between those two landmarks was a scattering of small shops and weathered bars separated by ageing homes, where it wasn't uncommon to find an old man or two, leaning against the wall smoking a pipe.

The journey from Belfast in Northern Ireland had been long and exhausting. There wasn't yet a major highway joining the North with the South then, and so the bus had travelled for hours along narrow winding roads. Farmers still marched their cattle from field to field on the laneways, often causing lengthy traffic jams, while potholes and black ice in some areas slowed vehicles almost to a standstill. At the beginning of their trip the brothers had engaged in lively chatter, but by the end the only thing either of them had to say was, 'Are we there yet?'

When at last they got to Stonebridge, they found a town quite out of step with the rest of the world, still working to the rhythm of an older Ireland. Being so close to Dublin, though, Stonebridge was already sprouting small housing estates that would inevitably become the commuter suburbs spreading out from Main Street.

'It's different,' commented Stephen with a faint laugh. 'Not like what we're used to back in Belfast!'

'You're telling me.' Dave took in the surroundings. 'It's so country-like, and everything's so small.'

'What do you think people do around here for fun?'

'Well, if it's not going to mass or the pub,' Dave sounded sarcastic, 'the only thing left is cow-tipping competitions, because God knows there's enough of them around here!' They'd passed through vast, lush farmland on the way.

'It's got to be a *village*!' announced Stephen suddenly. 'You couldn't call this place a town. It's definitely a village. There's hardly a building over two storeys high, and by the looks of things, *they're* pretty uncommon at that. Sure, look across the road!'

Dave took a quick glance and spotted the single petrol geyser, located on the footpath metres from the kerb, and directly in front of a single-storeyed pub.

'So much for petrol stations,' continued Stephen. 'Down here you can still pop into your local for a few pints and afterwards fill your car up before driving home!'

Dave laughed. 'You're some fool, you are.'

They were used to Belfast, the capital city of the Ulster province of Ireland. Dave could see it now in his mind's eye: flanked to the northwest by a series of hills, and resting at the mouth of the River Lagan, an expansive, high and heavily populated city. The skyline around their home was dominated by the huge gantry cranes of the famous Harland and Wolff dry shipping dock, and by imposing Edwardian-influenced buildings, some reaching eighty metres tall. From the Royal Courts of Justice to the grand Ulster Hall, Belfast was steeped in history, much of it identifiably British. But as well as busy streets and a sprawling mass of buildings, Belfast had a personality unlike anywhere else in Ireland.

David was only eight and Stephen six when the violence had erupted in the late sixties, invading their West-side home. From then on, the troubles in Northern Ireland had been deeply ingrained into their daily life. Not only segregated by walls or peace lines, the city was also scarred and in pain. Flags, graffiti and murals marked zones inhabited by 'West-side Catholics' or 'East-side Protestants', 'Republicans' or 'Loyalists'. Each neighbourhood had its own bars, its own organisations and, while many wanted to see harmony among all factions, there were those with enough power to steer things otherwise.

But it was only now that David had abruptly insisted they leave for Southern Ireland and take the bus ride to this small town on the River Liffey.

'I can't leave!' Stephen had yelled. 'There's too much going down here. And anyway, they'll hunt me down no matter where I am!'

'Believe me, Stephen, they've more chance of finding you here in Ulster than they do down South. You can't stay, I'm not going to let you. We're leaving tomorrow.'

'But what about Mammy and Francie, are we just going to disappear and say nothing to them?'

Dave shrugged his shoulders and sighed. 'Stephen, I warned you to keep your nose clean and not to get involved. I told you a million times, keep to yourself ...'

Stephen turned away. 'Don't you start lecturing me, Davie. You've made your point over and over again: no fucking lectures!'

'Well, stop all the excuses then. Do you think I want

to move? I sure as hell don't. I'm doing this to get you out of the mess you're in.' Dave took a breath, feeling distress, apprehension and anger. 'I've already told Francie what we're up to, and we'll write to Mammy when we're settled in Stonebridge. Maybe if things calm down up here, we can come back and visit her.'

The bus they travelled on was no longer in sight and the brothers were still familiarising themselves with their new home. 'Are you not cold?' asked Dave now. It was chilly and Dave was pleased that he'd worn a heavy jumper, unlike Stephen who stood strong in his flimsy white grandfather shirt.

'No. I'm not feeling a bit of it!'

Dave wasn't sure why he bothered asking: even if Stephen was cold, he would never admit to it. He was always too proud to admit weakness. Dave could see goose bumps along his arms, but Stephen said nothing of it.

Instead, as always, he grew impatient. 'All right then, so where is this guy?'

'He'll be here any minute, hold your horses!'

'And you're sure he's the real deal?'

'I'm positive, he's best mates with my old boss — he said Johnny'd set us up with a place to stay and a job, starting first thing.'

Stephen thought for a moment. 'What kind of job?'

Dave rolled his eyes. 'What do you care? We'll do whatever we have to do.'

'I suppose.'

An awkward silence followed and Dave took a deep sigh. He knew that it would be some time before Stephen accepted this new life; it wasn't going to be a smooth transition, but it was how things had to be.

Johnny was a short, stubby man with red blotchy cheeks and a rapidly receding hairline that he combed over. His overgrown grey moustache was very prominent on his round face and his thin beady eyes were dark and unemotional.

'It's a pretty nice place you've got here,' said Stephen as Johnny showed the two brothers around his house.

'It was left to me by my father when he passed away last year. It's old but I like it. You can stay until you find yourself something better.'

'It's great,' remarked Dave, relieved. They could lie low here, and hopefully start a new life.

It was a basic cottage, two miles outside of Stonebridge, deeply embedded in the green countryside. The layout was simple: the kitchen and living room were one room at the back of the house, from which a dimly lit hallway ran towards the front door. A bedroom was located on either side of the hallway; neither seemed favoured by the sun, but both were of a reasonable size. The toilet was in a small shed in the backyard — Johnny didn't look like the sort of man who had money to spare for renovations.

'Where's your bath?' asked Stephen.

Johnny threw some coal on the living room fire and then pointed to a steel bucket that sat on the floor beneath the kitchen sink. 'I use that for having a scrub,' he said.

'You don't have a bath?' Stephen was surprised.

'No!' replied Johnny. 'There's a drain on the floor beside the sink, you wash over the drain and then mop up what's left of the water when you're finished.'

'Are you serious?' Stephen stared at the bucket. 'I didn't think anyone washed themselves like that any more, not in Ireland anyway!'

Dave smiled teasingly at his brother. 'Stephen, looks like we're going to see that big willy of yours, after all. God knows you've been boasting about it for years!'

Stephen was unimpressed.

'Look, I know that it's not ideal,' interrupted Johnny, 'but it's better than nothing. And at least we're not like the French.' He began to chuckle. 'Those Frenchies never wash!' A moment of silence followed, before both brothers broke into laughter.

Having seen the house, they fetched their baggage into the bedroom.

'I'll take the window side,' Stephen quickly announced to Dave as he flung his suitcase across the room onto the bed.

Two single beds, one netted curtain over the window, a portrait of the crucifixion of Jesus on the wallpapered wall and an old, sturdy wardrobe in the corner — the room was otherwise bare. Stephen lay face up on the bed for a moment as Dave began to unpack his bag.

'That guy would give you the creeps, wouldn't he?' Stephen was looking intently at the portrait on the wall. 'I mean, who in their right mind wants a picture of a man wearing a crown of thorns with blood running down his face? You're taking a picture of somebody minutes before they die a horrible death and then framing it and putting it on your wall!'

'You'll go to hell,' mocked Dave. 'Don't let the priests hear you saying something like that.'

'Really, though, would you put something like that up on your wall?'

Dave nodded his head. 'Old people put those sorts of pictures up. It was probably Johnny's mam.'

'Who does Johnny remind you of?' Stephen quizzed.

'I don't know.' Dave wasn't interested. 'He's just your average man.'

'No,' continued Stephen in a whisper, 'he's got that look, that dirty-old-man look.'

'Give it a rest, Stephen!'

'No, I can just see him in his blue shitheap of a Datsun, pulling up beside a little boy who's making his way home from school and offering him sweeties if he climbs in the car!'

'He's harmless,' said Dave. 'He's a simple man. He doesn't seem to be the brightest but, you know, overall I think he's a gentle soul.'

Silence again. Stephen was unsettled.

'I can't believe we're down South,' he suddenly said, sitting up on the bed. 'Belfast is only up the road but it may as well be a million miles away now!'

'You're preaching to the converted, Stephen.' Dave continued unpacking. 'This is the last place I thought I'd be.'

'I'd say Francie was pissed.'

'I don't know.'

'I thought you told her what we were doing?' Stephen was surprised.

'She wasn't at home when I popped round, so I left her a note.'

'A *note*.' Stephen's voice rose. 'Are you crazy?'

'It was the best I could do, there was so little time.'

Frances was their older and only sister and Dave knew too well how furious she would be. She was far too sensible to comprehend how people could get themselves so deeply in strife. She would think it absurd to have resort to such extreme measures as moving away from home. Who would want to leave home when home was where Mammy was?

Their father had died young, and since then life had revolved around Mammy. She'd always been a domineering mother, but her dependence on her children after her husband's death was greater than ever. This firm hold might even have resulted in Stephen getting so heavily involved in the troubles.

Kept a child too long at his mammy's whim, Stephen's first decision as a twenty-one-year-old man had been to attend a so-called secret meeting, which transpired to be a pint of lager with three men in a known Catholic pub in central Belfast. The men were active members of a paramilitary group and their faces were extremely familiar to the residents of Stephen's neighbourhood.

'How could you meet with them?' shouted Francie soon after, unable to hide her disgust.

'I didn't meet with them, I don't know what you're talking about.' Stephen acted surprised.

Francie took a deep breath and, in a controlled manner, replied, 'Don't you dare lie to me, Stephen. Do you take me for a fool?' Francie was a slender, dark-haired woman, neat and conservative unlike her brothers. Her reserved nature cast an impenetrable hardness upon her personality. Her eyes were always cool and commanding, and she very rarely let down her guard. She was five years older than Stephen and had adopted the responsibilities that came with being the oldest child, sharing equally with their mammy total authority over her brothers. 'Did you think that no one would spot you?' she continued. 'That blabbering mouths wouldn't spread the word? Everyone in town knows what you're up to! What's Mammy going to say?'

'Who cares?' Stephen lowered his eyes.

Francie stepped back in astonishment. She had the look of somebody who's just stubbed their little toe on the corner of the bed — that same shrill of pain and the disbelief on her furrowed brow.

'It'll be you who cares the day you find her dead of a broken heart!'

Stephen looked away; it was easier to block out any distracting voices. What I'm doing is of more importance than Mammy, he thought.

Soon after, Francie spilled the beans to Dave.

Getting settled in Johnny's house was simple; getting used to Johnny was an entirely different task.

'It's like living in an army barracks,' grumbled Stephen one morning. 'Does he have to do everything so regimental-like?'

'I thought you'd be happy with that way of living, especially being a soldier of Ireland and all.'

Stephen bristled. 'Don't be a bollix!' he replied. 'You know what I mean; Johnny runs this house like it's boot camp!'

Each morning at exactly six o'clock Johnny would pound on the brothers' bedroom door.

'Hope you boys are awake,' he'd yell and then plant his ear against the door until he heard movement. By the time they emerged for breakfast, after twenty or so minutes of snooze, he'd be stripped and lathering his body in the kitchen. It wasn't a pretty sight. The early winter mornings were bitterly cold, which turned Johnny's white skin to an unhealthy shade of blue. As he spilled lukewarm water over himself and scrubbed his fragile-looking skin with carbolic soap, he looked surprisingly comfortable with his portly nakedness.

'Does he have to do this every morning?' moaned Stephen under his breath. 'I think I've seen enough bum crack to last me a lifetime.'

'I know.' Dave looked at his breakfast. 'It doesn't add much flavour to these eggs.'

Johnny would wash until the clock on the wall reached exactly six thirty, when he'd disappear into his bedroom. Moments later he would resurface, fully dressed and ready to commence his day as a council worker.

'All right, lads, time we hit the road and filled a few holes,' he'd announce at exactly six thirty-nine with a grin on his face. The boys would rise reluctantly from the table and follow him to the front door.

'Don't you eat?' inquired Dave one day.

'Are you joking me, of course I do. Sure I get up at five thirty every morning and have my porridge over and done with before I come anywhere near your door to wake you boys up!'

But Stephen had never liked being rushed; he hated anyone standing over him and telling him what to do. He especially hated their exact six forty departure time. Once, before he knew Johnny better, he answered back.

'I'm finishing my tea, give me a few minutes, will ye?'

Johnny smiled oddly and slowly approached Stephen, who sat up in his chair, caught slightly off guard.

'Stephen, I'm a little fat man,' he said, which made Stephen laugh. 'It's as well you may laugh,' continued

Johnny, suddenly very serious. 'I'm fat, I'm balding and I'm not the smartest man on the planet. I can't do anything about all of that, but one thing I can control is my job and likewise yours.' Stephen began to turn red in the face, but Johnny spoke further. 'I respect the fact that I am fortunate enough to be able to work, and so should you. I'll say this to you once and once only: if you want to keep your job, you'll drink that down now and get your arse out the door.'

Johnny wasn't their boss, he was simply the man who'd pulled a few strings to get them both a job with the local council — but clearly those strings could be cut at any time. After his little speech, Stephen and Dave never took him for granted.

As for the job, it was nothing glamorous, simply a means of making some money to pay for food and rent and have a little left over for a couple of beers of a night.

'Council workers!' declared Stephen on their first day. 'We're council bloody workers.'

'What's the matter with that?' said Dave as he put his fluorescent safety jacket on. 'It's better than nothing.'

Stephen wasn't convinced. 'Come on, Dave, it's as dumb as you can get. I mean, we're not talking brain surgery here now, are we?'

'I never knew you were a surgeon, Stephen. When

did this happen?' Dave smirked, but Stephen wasn't bothered.

'Come on, you've heard all the jokes. *How many council workers does it take to fill a hole? One to fill it and five to supervise.* That's us, we're those people now. We're the ones standing on the side of the road in the middle of winter with our arse cracks showing, a shovel in one hand and a Thermos of tea in the other. We're the lowest common denominator.'

'Well, try wearing a belt, stop you getting frostbite on that arse of yours.'

Stephen shook his head despondently. 'It's beneath us, you know it is.'

It angered Dave to hear Stephen talking like that, though he knew that his younger brother was still frustrated by their sudden flight from Belfast. 'Stephen, just get on with it, we're lucky to have anything. And anyway, working in a factory in Belfast wasn't a whole lot more interesting.'

'Well, hopefully it's just short-term.' He had to have the last word.

Johnny, on the other hand; he had absolute satisfaction in his daily toil.

'You'd swear it was a woman you were with by the way you're sticking your shovel in that hole!' one of the other workers once jibed him.

'You should watch and learn,' replied Johnny, 'maybe then you could give your missus something to talk about.' Johnny had been working with the council for years and was quick with a reply when he thought his work was under scrutiny. Not that it ever was: all the men knew of the care and precision he put into everything he did.

'I love it, I love everything about working in the outdoors. It doesn't get much better than this,' he often said. Johnny lived an otherwise simple life and were it not for his new housemates, he would spend most of it alone.

'Does he have a girlfriend?' Stephen asked one of the other crew.

The man gasped a pretend-shocked laugh. 'Are you joking, he's a bender.'

'A what?'

'A bender, a homosexual.'

'A homosexual. Really?' Stephen eyed Johnny, who was sipping on his morning tea in the makeshift hut they'd erected at the side of the road. The hut was lined in sheets of bright orange, casting an eerie glow over him.

'I'll grant you that he looks fucking weird drinking that tea there … but,' he thought for a second, 'are you sure he's gay? He doesn't look it.'

'That's what I've been told.'

Stephen glanced over at Johnny again and shook his head, unconvinced. Johnny must have sensed he was being watched and suddenly darted his eyes around, catching Stephen's. Stephen didn't flinch.

'What are you staring at?' Johnny called out as he took the last sip of tea from his steel cup.

'I'm trying to decide if you're gay or not.'

Silence broke like a thunder-clap. The other men continued to work, each alert to the conversation that was unfolding.

Despite only having spent a short time with Stephen, Johnny was already familiar with his brash and often uninformed statements.

Still, for a man who normally had a comment about everything, he was caught. His pale complexion turned a worrying grey.

'Have I offended you, Johnny?' Stephen finally continued, having received a disappointed look from Dave.

'No,' Johnny replied quietly. 'No, you haven't, Stephen — and you're about the only one here who hasn't.'

An audible grumble of disapproval fell from among the other workers like clay into the torn-up road.

'Yea, you all heard me,' Johnny suddenly exclaimed aloud. 'Talking behind my back all this time, thinking I didn't know what you were saying.'

The other men busied themselves with their work; guilt is often a pill best washed down with distraction.

'I'm not,' he continued. 'Just so you all know, I'm not!'

Johnny could describe the flaws and peculiarities of his co-workers, the secrets that he knew, but never spoke of, out of respect for the men he worked with every day. He could have made an example, to everyone, of just how it felt to be gossiped about in public, or behind your back. But that wasn't Johnny.

He chose instead to let the matter drop, but later, when night had fallen and the events of the day had passed, Johnny spoke with Stephen.

'This is all I've got, you know?'

Stephen looked away from the television screen that had drugged him into an evening of lounging on the chair for four hours, only rising once to go to the toilet.

'My dad got sick when I was about eighteen, he was fairly much bedridden after a stroke and Mam couldn't face dealing with a sick husband. She said it was too difficult to see him like that … It's not as though he chose to get sick, to spite her or something.'

Stephen sat up from a lazy slouch, his interest level raised.

Johnny continued. 'She moved in with her sister and left me to look after Dad — it took every free minute I had.' Johnny looked away forlornly. 'Dad didn't last very long, six months and he was gone. When Mam realised she'd lost the only thing of any importance in her life, she moved back home and became a recluse. So I looked after her too.'

Stephen was slightly confused by Johnny choosing to share this with him. Dave was the good listener, Dave was the responsible one, why wasn't Johnny talking to *him*?

'I never had time for women. I worked all day and took care of Mam the rest of the time. She lived for twelve years in her bedroom, never once did she leave except the day she was carried away in a box.' Johnny lifted his voice. 'So you see, I lost the chance to find a girl and I'm too old to be chasing after somebody. Now I'm happy with my job and with my house, anything else is just too complicated.'

Stephen's mind was doing somersaults trying to find something insightful to say, but Johnny saved him the effort.

'You don't have to say anything, it's no problem really. I just thought I'd let you know, since you're the only one who's ever had the courtesy not to talk behind my back.'

Johnny rose, stood there for a moment still deep in thought. Finally he turned towards the door.

'Switch off the light on your way to bed.'

Stephen watched as Johnny left the room. The faint murmur of the television lingered in the background but Stephen's mind was elsewhere. Suddenly, he was seized by a revelation and rose energetically to his feet.

'Fuck this, I'm out to find myself a woman.'

Grabbing his leather coat, he marched for the front door and, with a thud, left the house.

A week passed and at last it got the better of Dave's curiosity.

'Where have you been going every night?'

Stephen grinned cheekily. 'I was wondering when you'd ask me.'

'So? What's your story?'

Stephen looked very proud of himself. 'I've been seeing someone. A girl, and for your information a very beautiful girl, at that. I knew there was a reason for us to leave Northern Ireland.'

'Aside from the trouble you were in, of course?'

A tense moment followed. 'Thanks for reminding me.' Stephen became quiet and Dave suddenly felt guilty.

'So what's she like, this girl of yours?' Dave's voice had softened. He never liked being the older of them, it often forced him to a place of maturity that he didn't want to be in. He never wanted to be the one who was telling Stephen what was the right and wrong thing to do, he preferred to get involved in activities rather than adjudicate them. But what Stephen had been involved with back home was too serious to take lightly and Dave often felt he needed to remember that.

'She's gorgeous,' exclaimed Stephen enthusiastically. 'But I'm not telling you her name, it's none of your business.'

January 1990

'I categorically disagree with what you're suggesting,' a well-spoken British voice bellowed on the radio. '*It astounds me to hear you say that Ireland is still at war. It's quite the opposite. In fact, I'd go so far as to say that, right now, Ireland is the closest it's ever been to reaching a peaceful reconciliation with the United Kingdom. Please God the shameful days of bombings by the IRA are now at an end.*'

'By *the IRA?*' another voice interrupted, this time strongly accented, from Northern Ireland. '*That's all you ever talk about. It'll take more than the IRA to end all this violence and you know that well. Coming on this radio station and making claims that the troubles in Ireland are nearing an end because the IRA have laid down their arms is irresponsible.*'

'*Irresponsible? I don't think there's anything*

irresponsible about signalling an end to all the carnage.'

'Yes, but implying that only the IRA can put an end to it is wrong. What about the Ulster Defence Force, the Orange Marches — there's two sides to every war. If it's so close to an end, go tell the Protestants that they can't march through Catholic neighbourhoods this year —'

Susan stood up abruptly. 'I can't stand listening to it,' she exclaimed, flicking the dial until static and fuss was replaced by music.

A knock sounded on the back door, startling her.

As she swung it open, cold night air invaded the house.

'Electricity meter!' exclaimed a teenage boy, rugged up against the evening cold.

Susan let him in and watched as he unlocked the electricity meter box and poured its contents into his hand. There was hardly any money in it. It was embarrassing enough that the house was still using a paid electrical meter box let alone the fact that at some point years earlier, Dave had found a way of using a magnet to slow up the meter's revolutions and had reduced the cost significantly.

'There's not much here,' commented the boy, as they sometimes did.

Susan blushed but the young boy with the acne face and the barely formed moustache wasn't overly concerned. He shrugged his shoulders resolutely before placing the money in his pocket and heading for the door. 'All right, missus, have a good night, *tank* you!' He shut the door behind him as he left and the heat from the fire began to restore warmth to the house.

She could hear the overworked and injured top-loading washing machine in high rotation, as it completed the last cycle of a wash. There was a constant clanking of something metal inside the machine and Susan decided that it was the wearing and tearing of her new black bra as its fasteners scraped along the inside of the machine.

There goes my last hope for some romance, she thought, my cheap Penny's bra being thrashed about in the washing machine.

Susan had just turned thirty when she moved into this house and since then she often felt that she'd aged terribly.

I'm starting to look more and more like my grandmother every day, she'd think, investigating her slender face for the onset of wrinkles. Next thing my boobs will drop and it'll be lights out for me. Staring at herself in the mirror with disappointment, she'd wonder, Where's Susan gone to?

Susan had never been shy of flirting with men. She was easy on the eye: her full lips were both sensuous and refined and her long red hair glinted. She had a fine slender body with well-proportioned breasts and a pinchable behind, but her most alluring feature was her apparent innocence: her strict upbringing had marked her forever with an air of naivety — which was at times disarming in the light of her true personality.

To suggest that Susan had developed into something of a wild girl was incorrect; she simply had abundant love and excitement for living life to its fullest. In her twenties she'd rarely concerned herself with possible outcomes, but instead had lived in the here and now, and so she had developed a bit of a reputation.

At the factory where she'd worked, a rumour had circulated that Susan was having sex with one of the other employees. It was said that one evening after work, when most people had left, Susan had signalled Christy Flynn to meet her in the boss's office, and that on entering he'd found her undressed and waiting for him. It was also rumoured that Christy wasn't the only person to receive such an invitation.

'You're nothing but a floozy!' Her father had launched straight in, when word got back to him. 'I've heard all about you and your antics at work. You're a *whore.*' The town rumours were damning by now, and not what he expected from the daughter of a man of his station. He wasn't wealthy but he had more than many others, and believed that such things didn't happen in the echelons of society to which he aspired.

'It's all lies,' she fought back. 'People are just making up stories about me, I never did anything like that! Christy has been asking me out for months and I've been saying no every time — it wouldn't surprise me if he started the rumour.'

'I don't believe you. I've always known that you were nothing but a tramp — now the whole town knows.'

'Believe what you want to believe.' She headed for the door. 'I'm not seventeen now, I don't have to listen to my bigot father any more!'

She wasn't a whore and she knew it. She'd done nothing wrong and if her attitude to life was so threatening to people that they'd spread scurrilous tales about her, well bad luck to them. Even if the rumours had been true, Susan saw no harm in it. She didn't credit what she regarded to be the prudish and God-fearing boundaries of Catholic Ireland.

'Life is for the living,' she'd cried out as she left the house, slamming the door behind her.

Now, years later, she lived with her nine-year-old nephew. She and Mattie were still getting to know each other, and she often needed her own space, quiet time to herself to collect her thoughts. She was lonely and at times troubled. Most importantly, thought Susan, he knew that his aunty was very fond of him, perhaps even loved him. Mattie's own mood could change suddenly; one minute he'd be happy, the next he'd be fussing about washing his plate after dinner or putting the toilet seat down when he'd finished, or not going to bed.

Susan looked at her watch and then shook her head disapprovingly. Tonight Mattie was late — and so was Dave, for that matter.

When Mattie had come down for his breakfast that morning, he'd patted his gelled hair, catching Susan's eye — who had been reluctant to comment about it before.

'Yes, nice job, I see you've been at your dad's hair gel?'

Mattie bowed his head with embarrassment.

'Honestly it looks very good,' she continued, seeing his uneasiness. 'I like how you've —' She searched to find the right word and then, gesturing, she continued '— pressed it so close to your head like that!'

Though Mattie had been in front of the bathroom mirror for ages, a flat mass of black strands was pasted to his skull as though someone had ironed his hair that way.

'It's how I like it,' he replied defensively. 'It's cool!'

'I think it's great … In fact, I think we could use it for something else.' She neared him and, from above, peered down onto his shiny head. 'Yes, I was right, we could use it for a mirror, as well!'

Mattie turned to look at her with astonishment: was she telling the truth?

'Really?' he said, deflated.

She hadn't the heart to continue the charade. 'Of course not, silly,' she said as she began to run her fingers through the congealed paste in his hair. 'But maybe we could give it a little bit of life, lift it up …'

Mattie didn't stop her.

'There you go,' she concluded with a light tap on his shoulders. 'Now you'll impress that girlfriend of yours.'

'Girlfriend,' he proclaimed with a lift in his voice. 'I don't have a girlfriend, there's no one I fancy!'

'Maybe it's a boyfriend then?' she teased.

'Don't be stupid, Aunty Susan! Why would I want a boyfriend for and I especially don't want a girlfriend. Girls are thick.'

Now Susan smiled, thinking about the Brylcreem. What am I going to do with him? she thought. There was clearly *someone* to impress. And tears began to streak the make-up down her face.

'Oh God.' She shook herself, trying to loosen the thoughts circling in her head. Then she opened the back door and stepped out onto the icy porch. 'I can't believe I've got to resort to this,' she moaned. She used to hate hearing parents do this kind of thing. She took a reluctant breath and then at the top of her lungs yelled out, 'Mattie, Mattie Finch, come home for your dinner!'

Fog had settled in: the air was thick and heavy. Susan's voice got absorbed into the night, swallowed up by the sounds of the streets as the cars drove by, chewed up by the multitude of conversations bouncing from wall to wall in the lines of joined houses. The mish-mash of sounds only added a sense of futility to Susan's mission but even so, she decided to try one more time. 'Mattie Finch, come home for your —'

'Dinner!' It was Dave. His unmistakeable Northern voice came first, then he emerged from the blanket of mist. Susan leapt back in surprise.

'Oh Jesus Christ, you scared the life out of me!' she almost shrieked. 'Don't do that again, do you hear me, don't do that again.'

'Sorry, Susan,' he laughed softly and approached her, his arms outstretched.

Susan had contemplated this for some time, the moment they would meet again. She had decided it would be best if they didn't hug. I can be polite, she had told herself, I can shake hands and make small talk, but that's it. Too much has happened, I can't let him think that I forgive him for everything that June had to go through. That wouldn't be fair on her.

But now she had little choice and, in the end, to hug felt like the natural thing to do. And in his warm embrace, she realised that she was in need of this, it had been months since they'd last met. Despite all his failings, she still had an undeniable fondness for the pale-skinned man with the silver hair and the cleanly shaven face. She was being reunited with an old friend.

Dave released her from his arms and under the faint porch light watched as Susan brushed tears from her eyes. Dave's heart sank.

'Are you all right?' he whispered, resting his hands on her shoulders and staring into her eyes. Susan glanced towards the next-door neighbours'. She never liked speaking outdoors; you never knew who could hear you.

'It's been hard,' she replied softly, collecting herself as she spoke and wiping the tears from her face. 'It's been so hard!'

'I know,' said Dave before hugging her again. 'I'm so sorry!'

Dave held Susan until she was ready to let go.

Finally she stepped back and, with a sniff, said, 'Come in out of the cold.'

She felt a little vulnerable for having cried in front of Dave and decided to distract herself by filling the kettle and putting it to the boil. Dave knew she needed a moment and left the room to hang his jacket in the closet under the stairs, before retreating to the living room and sitting down. Through the open door there, he could see Susan in the kitchen. An awkward silence had developed between them. It's only to be expected, he thought.

Susan poured hot water into two mugs, the tea bags bobbing up and down as they filled.

Dave was gazing around the living room. He felt like he'd slipped backwards in time.

In every direction there was a memory, some fragment of his past. This was the room where he and June had spent the majority of their time together. They'd laughed and cried, they'd fought and made up, they'd shared hopes and dreams and faced loss and disappointment. Dave approached the television that rested on a brown wooden cabinet at the back of the room. He grinned. 'The biggest purchase of our lives,' he murmured, remembering how he and June had deliberated for weeks over purchasing such an expensive item.

'We're barely scraping by,' June had argued for the fiftieth time. 'Why do we need to spend the little bit that we have on a colour television?'

'For comfort,' replied Dave. 'If we have to stay in every night, we may as well have a decent television to look at!'

'All right, I'm convinced,' she'd finally announced with a smile. 'It's good to talk about these things first, that's all.'

The following weekend the television had arrived and, excitedly, they unpacked it together and propped it up on the cabinet. Dave switched it on and stepped back. There was only snow.

'Em,' he said, pondering, and then proceeded to fiddle with the dials. 'Probably needs tuning.'

June had left him alone to work on it, but when she returned later she was surprised to see that the situation hadn't improved. 'No luck, eh. Maybe you need to put an aerial in it,' she said, laughing.

'It didn't come with one ... I think it's built in.' Dave scratched his head and turned the dials one more time.

'Come here,' she said, her hands hidden behind her. 'Give me a kiss and it'll be all better.'

'What's behind your back!' jibed Dave, and he began to kiss June playfully while intentionally groping her backside.

With a swift movement, June freed herself from Dave's embrace and plunged the steel coat hanger into the aerial port of the television.

'*Ta-da*,' she exclaimed with a wave and a cheeky smile on her face. Sound and picture resonated from the television and Dave turned to his wife and grinned. 'So you're not just an extremely pretty face, after all,' he replied, kissing her again and pinching her behind one last time.

And now, eight years on, the television was still in the same spot, the twisted coat hanger still acting as a receiver. I really should have got a proper aerial, thought Dave. Actually I probably should have got a new television by now too.

Susan called from the kitchen. 'Do you want sugar in your tea?'

Dave didn't answer: something else had caught his attention. The simple painting on the wall just above the television was in bright watercolours, washed together to form a fruit bowl. In the bottom right corner, *June Finch 1 of 1* was signed in black charcoal.

'Why one of one?' Dave had asked when June waved the painting in front of him, wanting to know what he thought of it. Mattie was only three years old at the time, and she'd decided to use their living room as a painter's studio, to entertain the little lad. Already there was paint everywhere, on the couches, on the floor, on June, and not to mention the mosaic of colours that Mattie had succeeded in getting all over himself.

'One of one will increase the value of it when I'm a hugely successful artist,' said June. 'Just imagine, in years to come, when some rich old lady stumbles across it in an art gallery — well, she'll nearly have a heart attack; who would believe it, a June Finch original!'

'Ah, I see.' Dave nodded. 'Then maybe I should buy it off you now while you're still fairly much unknown. It could be my retirement fund.'

'Maybe you should,' she teased.

Dave looked properly at the painting. 'It's great, June … I didn't know that you painted.'

'Ah, don't be silly,' she said bashfully. 'It's only a fruit bowl, nothing amazing.'

'No, it's great, honestly.' He looked closer at one of the fruits in the centre of the bowl. 'The banana looks like it's seen better days, though!'

'It's an orange!' exclaimed June.

'An orange, really?'

'Does it not look like one?' She was suddenly serious, and Dave realised that he'd put his foot in his mouth.

'I'm only having you on, of course it does. Actually, you know what I think we should do?' Dave turned to Mattie and lifted him into his arms. 'Me and my little man here should put it up on the wall, and I think that just above the TV will be a perfect spot for it.'

From the kitchen Susan called again, rousing Dave from his daydream. 'Sugar?'

'Yes, please, two!'

He hadn't noticed before, but there was the small, faint impression of Mattie's handprint just below the painting. He remembered how he'd sat the boy on the TV and asked him to hold the painting against the wall while he marked the place for a nail. Dave smiled. How much his son had grown since then.

As Susan brought the tea in, Dave was drawn to the dusty framed photographs on the mantelpiece. He lifted the largest of them in his hands.

'My God, you were so beautiful that day,' he sighed, seeing June beaming from ear to ear as she tried to pose while the wind blew her wedding veil in all directions. Dave was standing in the foreground of the picture, watching with pride as his new bride sparkled like no other.

'That's a great picture!' exclaimed Susan behind him.

Dave turned abruptly, 'Oh, you surprised me there.' He continued to look at the photo.

'The weather was much windier than June usually is,' commented Susan. 'We had about a hundred clips in her hair to keep that veil from taking flight.' She came closer to look at the picture. 'She was so happy that day!'

'So was I,' replied Dave, returning the photo to its dusty resting place.

'Here's your tea.'

Dave sat down, as did Susan. Silence followed.

Finally Dave made an attempt to break the awkwardness. 'So, where's Mattie?'

'Sometimes he likes to stay on at Niall's.'

'Oh.' Dave nodded again, still caught in the memories. 'It's very late, though!'

'It's not that late.' Susan was suddenly defensive. 'He's nine years old now and, given everything that has happened, I think it's probably a good thing if he's got some friends to take his mind from it all.'

Silence followed again.

'I wasn't having a go, Susan. I'm sorry.'

'So are you sober?' Susan's words were like poison in Dave's gullet. He knew it was her right and responsibility to ask, he knew he had no reason to feel self-protective, but still it made him feel bad to hear the question.

'Six weeks now,' he replied, his head lowered.

'Six weeks.' Susan reflected. 'It's not very long … Are you sure you're ready to come back home?'

Dave sat up in his seat. 'I've been getting help. I'm done with it, Susan, it may as well be six years, I'll never touch another drink as long as I live. I miss my son too much.'

'He really needed you over the past six months.' Susan wasn't satisfied with his answer. 'It's taken you a long time to realise how much you missed him!'

Dave sipped from his tea and took a deep breath. It was important that he remain calm — Susan deserved that much at least, for all that she'd done for Mattie.

'You're right, Susan.' His voice was low and forlorn. 'I can't argue with that. I should have been here months ago.'

'You *were* here,' she interrupted. 'You were so drunk you probably don't remember it. I told you to come back when you were sober, and today is the first time that I've seen you since.'

Dave was cowed, he had no argument. 'I know, Susan, believe me, I know.' He sighed heavily. 'There's so many things that I've done wrong, but there was nothing I could do. I have an illness and now I'm dealing with it.'

'Illness? Cancer is an illness, drinking yourself to oblivion is just selfish greed.'

'It's an illness, Susan.' Dave was certain of this fact. 'Anyway, giving it a name doesn't change the fact that I let June and Mattie down. I've got to live with that.'

'They weren't the only ones you let down. You let yourself down.' There was so much she wanted to say to Dave, so many speeches she'd rehearsed in her head, but seeing the man now, with his shattered spirit, she knew that her words would only destroy him more. And Mattie needed him to be strong.

'Let's not talk about it any more,' she continued, 'just don't let me down.'

'I won't, Susan, I promise.'

'All right,' she concluded. 'Now, there's something you need to know, something about Mattie.'

Dave sat up. 'What is it, is he having trouble again at school?'

'No, although it's not doing him any favours there, either.'

'What is it? Tell me.'

'He's ...' she hesitated. 'He's been doing something that he shouldn't.' Again she halted.

'Say it, Susan, whatever it is just say it.'

'He's been talking to June.'

'He what?' Dave was shocked.

'He talks to her, every day — she walks him to school, they go places together.'

'Are you serious?'

'Do you think I'd joke about something like this?'

'But —' He was lost for words. 'But, he can't do that.'

Suddenly a noise from the back door shook them from their conversation.

'Shh. That'll be him now, we'll talk more about it later.' Dave was suddenly on edge and Susan could see it. 'Take it easy,' she urged. 'You need to be composed when he comes in.'

'Aunty Susan,' a voice yelled from the kitchen.

'I'm in the living room, Mattie.'

Seconds later the handle of the door turned and Mattie entered, fresh-faced and enthusiastic, his hair still gelled from the fun they'd had doing it this morning. He saw his father immediately.

'Dad!' he yelled out excitedly, running to his father with open arms. 'You're home!'

The boy threw himself into Dave's arms and held tight. He'd missed him. Tears welled in Dave's eyes and, for an instant, all the worries and doubts he had, all of the guilt that he carried around with him, dissolved.

Susan looked away. She couldn't decide whether she should stay in the room or give them some privacy.

Suddenly Mattie released his hold on his father and stared seriously into his eyes. 'Where did you go to?'

Dave looked at Susan.

'He was away, on work,' she cut in.

'For so long, you even missed Christmas!'

Dave frowned. 'Yea, yea, I know, son.'

'It was a hard one,' commented Susan under her breath, catching Dave's attention.

He replied, 'You can say that again.'

Mattie took a moment to think. 'And did you go to Africa?' His eyes were wide with curiosity.

'Africa?' Dave glanced at Susan, who was as puzzled as he was. 'What do you mean?'

'My friend at school's dad was like you, he had to go off working for a long time because he was in Africa, making gold.'

Dave cheered up; for a moment he'd thought his son was about to chastise him for his long absence. Instead he was excited to think that his father might have been somewhere exotic. Dave was about to answer but Mattie's form suddenly changed, as a thought crossed his mind.

'Mam said that you were a bad man.'

The words left his mouth so easily that it took Dave moments to comprehend what he'd just heard.

'What did she say?'

'She said that you were a bad man but then she changed her mind and said that you weren't really a bad man, you just weren't very good.'

'When did she say that?'

'When we left England without you.'

Dave felt a sudden lump in his throat. It was harder hearing those words coming from Mattie's mouth than if he'd heard them directly from June. It was crushing to hear his son speaking about him in such a way, even if he was only relaying a message.

'That's not a nice thing to say, Mattie,' scolded Susan, who was equally startled by his revelation.

'But it's what she said,' protested Mattie.

'Even still, it doesn't give you the right to repeat it. Your mam was probably angry with your dad.' Susan found she was defending Dave, much to her own surprise. 'I'm sure that she didn't mean what she said.'

'I know,' he continued excitedly, turning back to Dave. 'When we were *on* the boat she said that you were only bad when you were drunk. All the rest of the time she said that you were the best man in the world.'

Dave was overcome by an instant rush of emotion. 'Did she really say that?' He no longer cared about the *bad man* comment, it was the compliment that had touched him deepest. A compliment from the woman he loved more than anything else, a simple string of words that told him that she didn't think he was a loser. Maybe he wasn't the worst thing that ever happened to such a beautiful woman, after all. He'd told himself the opposite for so long that it had become a fact in his mind.

'Yea, that's what she said.'

Dave threw his arms around his son one more time. He could have stayed like that forever, but Mattie, being only nine years old, had small tolerance for hugging and stuff like that and managed to wriggle his way out of the embrace. 'Dad,' he moaned, 'you're gonna break my back.'

'Sorry,' said Dave, throwing a glance at Susan. 'Already too old for a cuddle; where have the years gone?'

'Have a look at the lines on my face and you'll see where the years are gone.'

'Would you go on out of that — since I've known you, you haven't changed a pick.'

Susan blushed. 'So,' she said as a distraction, 'have you got any clothes with you or did the African lions eat them all?'

'Did you see lions?' Mattie's eyes lit up.

'No,' replied Dave to Mattie, 'unfortunately I didn't see any lions; but yes, Susan, I've got some bits and pieces with me. I left my suitcase outside, in case you'd changed your mind and decided not to let me in.'

'It's your house,' said Susan, 'you could come home whenever you wanted.'

'Well,' replied Dave, clapping his hands together and trying to maintain a cheery tone, 'I'm here now, which is what really matters.' He stood up. 'Come on outside, Mattie, and help me with my bags.'

The two left the room, chatting as they went. Susan began to tidy up and, with the hum of the evening news on the television and the crackling of coal on the fire, a sense of the old days began returning to the house.

'Stephen isn't safe.'

Dave listened to his sister Francie as she spoke over the phone in distress.

'What do you mean, what have you heard?'

The phone went silent. Dave could hear Francie breathing, each breath broken slightly by the crying she was trying so hard to conceal.

'Don't cry, Francie,' urged Dave. 'It's going to be all right, I'm looking out for him.'

'It's not as simple as that, they're coming down South to get him, they know where you're living.'

Dave suddenly felt a heightened awareness of his surroundings: the exposed phone box that he was standing in, the quiet side street where it was situated, the two burly men standing at the end of the road smoking cigarettes and chatting.

'Are you still there?' Her voice sounded stressed and anxious. Francie rarely lost her composure and she hardly ever cried. Dave remembered the last time he'd seen her truly upset; it was at their father's funeral. The suddenness of his death didn't leave much time for coming to terms with the loss. There was the coffin to buy, the funeral to arrange, there were the sandwiches and the tea and the pints of stout for the family and friends who were all to be invited back after the ceremony. There was Mammy.

'I will look after everything!' Francie swore to their mother, who was overcome with grief. 'Don't you worry about a thing, we'll make sure that Daddy has a proper send-off.'

Dave and Stephen offered to do their share also but she wouldn't have any of it.

'Come on, Francie, let me do something.' Dave had protested.

'No, I told Mammy that I will arrange everything and that's exactly what I'm going to do.' She took a quick look at Stephen, whose eyes were red from crying. It had hit him hard. Francie shook her head sadly and then turned back to Dave. 'Sure, our Stephen's no use to anyone, you're best seeing that he's all right. Go and bring him out for a pint or something.'

She had never cried once in the days leading up to the funeral, and it wasn't until their father's wooden casket was being lowered into the lonely hole in the ground that she was finally confronted by what was happening.

'Stop what you're doing,' she cried, her loud voice crashing through the quiet air of Belfast's Milltown cemetery. 'This is a mistake, don't put my father in there, he's not dead.'

Dave would never forget the look of complete despair on her face, the horror of her eyes. And for months after that she could not show her face in public.

'Are you there?' she was repeating now on the other end of the phone.

'I'm still here,' replied Dave, holding the earpiece loosely against his skull. 'I'm thinking about it. Do you know who they've sent?'

'No!' The question angered her. 'How would I know that, that organisation has people all over the place. For all I know they could have somebody already down South, somebody you even might know.'

Dave bit his lip. 'Yea, you're right.'

Up ahead, somewhere in the distance, the uncomfortable sound of screeching car brakes filled the air — was it a threat?

'What's that sound?' quizzed Francie.

'Nothing to worry about,' he replied.

Dave gazed at the men smoking their cigarettes. He could have sworn they'd been further away from him earlier. Stonebridge was suddenly an unfamiliar place, a morass of danger and distress. Dave shook his head. I need to keep it together, he thought, scaring myself isn't going to help matters.

Dave examined the men again. They haven't moved, he reassured himself, that's exactly where they've been all the time.

'They'll kill you too!' Francie's voice jolted him.

'No, they won't.' Dave spoke with strained confidence. 'That's not going to happen, Francie, and you need to get a grip of yourself and stop thinking like this.'

At the end of the road, an old blue Fiat came struggling around the corner, stopping and starting like an elderly man climbing the stairs. The young learner gripped the steering wheel as though she was clinging to the edge of a cliff. Each time her foot landed nervously on the brake, it sent a painful screech into the afternoon air.

Everything will be fine, thought Dave, and feeling the need to console his sister, he repeated it aloud. 'You've got to stop worrying, Francie. Remember, you're the strong one. You're the one who keeps us all together, don't lose it now.'

Francie sniffled, happy with the accolade. 'I know, but I'm just so frightened for you both.'

'Everything will blow over, I promise you. Surely they've got to understand that Stephen didn't mean to do what he did, he was scared, he did what he thought was the best thing at the time.'

Stephen had told Dave what he'd done the night before they left Northern Ireland. Countless times since then Dave had made him go over the events that had forced them to flee. By now he knew the facts almost better than Stephen did.

'You what?' Dave had exclaimed that first time he'd heard it, horrified. 'You've kneecapped people?'

'You wouldn't understand,' replied Stephen in a whisper. The two brothers sat in the snug of an old man's pub, with two pints of Guinness close at hand.

'And that doesn't bother you, you can live with yourself? Thanks to you, some poor fucker will never walk again, you can sleep knowing that?'

Stephen looked at his brother with annoyance. 'I'm not here for a lecture, I'm here for your help. You asked how involved I was and I'm telling you. I'm not proud of what I've done but if you asked me would I do it again, I would. I believe in the Irish cause.'

'Well, I *don't*,' shouted Dave, then lowered his voice. 'It's all bollix, if you ask me. It's just a pack of hypocrites trying to keep a fight alive. Catholics and Protestants, it's all the same. All I know is that it's the innocent people who are always caught in the crossfire.' Dave shook his head in disbelief. 'It's all bullshit and nothing you're doing is ever gonna change things, you'll see, everything will stay the same. Northern Ireland will still be owned by the Queen of England.'

'How can you say that?' argued Stephen, shocked. 'Do you not know your history? The British came into our country and robbed us of everything we owned: our culture, our religion, our land. I can't call myself an Irishman if I'm not willing to stand up and fight for what is truly ours.'

'Yea, great speech, Stephen, but what a crock of shit,' interrupted Dave. 'I know my history probably better than you do and the things that you're talking about happened over a hundred years ago. We've still got our culture and enough religion to last a lifetime. Nowadays it's just Irishmen fighting Irishmen. You're not fighting the British any more.' Dave composed himself. 'Stephen, you know what? I've got to tell you, lately I've become so ashamed of you!'

Stephen's face dropped. 'Fuck you!'

'No, fuck *you*, Stephen, have you listened to yourself lately?' Dave leant across the table, he felt more in control that way. 'Have you stepped back for a minute and taken a good hard look at yourself? You're different! God knows that you've always had a chip on your shoulder, but now you're ready to take on the entire world.'

'That's rubbish!'

'Is it?' Dave paused. 'Do you think Mammy wants to hear you blabbering on every night over dinner about your *cause*? How do you think it makes her feel to know that her son has turned into a thug — and you and I both know that she only barely knows the half of it? She thinks you're just a sympathiser.'

'She never disagrees with anything that I'm saying.'

'That's because she's stopped trying to reason with you; you just wouldn't listen. You've shot her down so many times by talking back to her that she's frightened to open her mouth around you. She's an old woman, Stephen, a widow.'

Stephen didn't speak for a time, he knew his brother needed to calm down first.

Then, after a few moments, his words were crystal clear. 'Look, Dave, I need your help.'

'What have you done?' Dave sighed.

'Something stupid …' Stephen stared at his glass as though the solution to his problem was hidden somewhere on its smooth surface. 'Something really bloody stupid!'

'Stupider than kneecapping someone?' Dave's tone of incredulity was forbidding.

But Stephen glared at his brother. 'Yea, stupider than kneecapping.'

'Hit me with it, what happened?'

'You're not going to like this.'

'Just tell me, for God's sake!'

Stephen glanced subtly in all directions, suddenly cautious about being heard. Then, reassured, he began to speak softly. 'They were planning a bombing.'

'Of what?'

'A pub somewhere in town.'

Dave felt uneasy in his seat and he shivered at the thought.

'I wasn't involved at first,' continued Stephen. 'Actually I never thought I was involved at all. I just got a message that they needed somebody to do an errand, down South, a run across the border to pick up some things. So I put my hand up for the job.'

'Are you nuts?'

'Well, how was I to know what they wanted me to pick up?' Stephen said defensively. 'I've done tons of those trips and it's always been for documents or photographs. I didn't know they wanted me to bring explosives back across the border.'

Dave controlled his anger. 'So, what's happened?'

Stephen focussed on his beer once again; he found it hard to look Dave in the eyes. 'So I picked up the gear, and took off for Belfast.'

'Did you not check what it was?'

'No, not at first. It was just a sealed cardboard box, it looked like a standard package.' Stephen took a sip from his beer, catching a momentary glimpse of Dave's frustrated gaze. 'Anyway, when I was about half an hour from the border, as God is my judge, something made me pull the car over and open the box. Don't laugh when I say this, but I swear to God, I think it was *Dad* made me look.'

'Dad?' Dave was astonished.

'Yea, Dad. I know it sounds stupid, but — you remember how much he loved listening to Nat "King" Cole?'

Dave nodded.

'Well, "Unforgettable" came on the radio and it got me thinking about Dad and then seconds later I suddenly felt this major need to slam on the brakes and rip that box open. I'm serious, it was the strangest feeling.'

It was a lovely notion, but in the context of the conversation, Dave didn't want to entertain it. 'Stephen, this is a new low, speaking about our dead father like this, have you lost your mind entirely?'

'Look, I'm just telling you what happened. It makes no difference really, the main thing was that I had a bomb in the car and I knew instantly that I couldn't cross the border with it.'

'Because you wouldn't be part of a mass murder?'

Stephen looked away. 'No, I didn't want to get caught smuggling it and wind up going to gaol.'

Dave slammed his fist against the table. 'Stephen!'

'What?' He decided to fight back. 'What do you want from me, Dave? Stop being so high and mighty, so bloody pious. Would you just hear me out without all the dramatics?'

Dave wasn't interested, and stood up. 'I'm out of here, I don't care what sort of trouble you're in.'

'Wait!' Stephen grabbed hold of his wrist. 'Sorry, I didn't mean that, sit down and let me finish.'

Reluctantly, Dave sat down and Stephen began again. 'Once I decided I wasn't going to cross the border with the package, I ditched the car and the package and hitchhiked my way home.'

'Why did you do that? Why didn't you just ditch the package? You could still have driven home.'

Stephen sighed. 'Well, that's the fucking problem: I don't know why I didn't do that! I don't know what I was thinking. If I had driven home, then I'd be fine.'

'What do you mean?'

'Well, the night before I had to pick up the gear, I went out drinking. I was blind drunk and I woke up like the walking dead the next morning.' He took a tired breath. 'I was supposed to rob a car so the plates couldn't be traced to anyone, but when I woke up I was already hours late and I had no time. So I loaned a car belonging to one of the other boys. I knew he didn't need it and I figured I'd have it back before anyone would be the wiser.'

'Who is he, the guy who owns the car?'

'A man named Gerry Macklin. He's low rank in the organisation, but his father, Mick, is right up there, a serious player. He's a hard man.'

'Fuck, Stephen!' Dave knew what was coming next, he could hear the words in his head before Stephen uttered them. The car would have been found 'suspiciously abandoned' on the side of the road where he'd left it, and the police, being on high alert, would have traced the plates back to Gerry —

'Gerry's house got raided this morning and he's been taken away by the army.'

Dave felt livid. But at the same time, he had nothing

to say to Stephen. He was suddenly numb with the prospect of what was next for his brother if Mick caught up with him. Dave's eyes glazed over; what had happened to his brother, and to their relationship?

As children Dave and Stephen had been almost inseparable, spending every minute together. They had opposing personalities but it was their differences that seemed to strengthen their bond. Stephen was the volatile one, while Dave was the one most likely to apologise when he did something wrong. Stephen was impulsive and adventurous while Dave was quiet and cautious. They had a relatively happy childhood, but everything changed after the death of their father — including their relationship. No one knew for certain what had happened to their father but the most common explanation was that, like so many innocents in Northern Ireland, he'd wandered down the wrong street at the wrong time and become the victim of a mistaken identity. He was found dead, shot four times through the chest.

'That's it,' Stephen had said to Dave, just after the funeral, 'I'm joining the cause, I'm not going to just sit back and watch while innocent Catholics, just like our poor father, are being shot down in cold blood.'

'Don't get involved,' warned Dave. 'You don't know what happened to Dad: this might not have been paramilitary-related at all. How do you know what he was up to?' The words had just slipped from Dave's lips.

Stephen was confused. 'What's that supposed to mean? What are you implying?' His voice began to rise. 'Are you saying that he deserved this?'

Dave turned to leave the room. He couldn't have this discussion with Stephen. He had said too much already; and anyway, it broke his heart to talk like that of his father — even though he knew a little more about him than his brother did.

'You think that Daddy deserved to die? For what, Dave? For *what*?' Stephen yelled after him.

But as far as Dave was concerned, the discussion was over. And though both men apologised later, the distance had been set between them then, and it would never be closed.

On their last night in Northern Ireland, Stephen had sipped again from his pint. 'I really am in a lot of trouble.'

'I know.' Dave was deep in thought. 'And it's got nothing to do with the IRA, it's between you and Gerry's father.'

Stephen bowed his head. 'They told me to get out of town.'

'What?'

'A man stopped me outside the pub. He had a gun.' Stephen paused. 'Three days, three fucking days is all I've got left.'

Suddenly Stephen was on the verge of losing control.

For an instant, Dave saw Stephen as his vulnerable little brother again, the five-year-old boy on his first day at school looking to his older brother to show him around. The situation now for Stephen couldn't have been any worse.

'We're out of here. First thing tomorrow morning, we'll head down South.'

'But we can't, where will we go, what will we do? What about Mammy?'

'I'll talk to a friend of mine, he'll get us a job. Leave that to me. You go hide somewhere. Don't go back home, kid, don't go anywhere near home.'

'But Mammy, what about her?'

'Stephen, if you go around home, you're a dead man. First things first, let's look after you. We'll sort out everything else later.'

Stephen shook his head in disbelief, puffing a breath of air as he ran his hand through his ruffled hair. He tried to argue again.

'Stephen!' Dave regarded him sternly. 'It's what it is. You've got yourself in this mess and you'll need to face up to it pretty fast, because it's not going away in a hurry!'

Now, in Stonebridge, standing at the phone box talking to his sister Francie, Dave was feeling the same sense of responsibility charging through him.

The two men smoking the cigarettes had gone indoors and the learner in the blue Fiat had safely parked her car. But Francie was becoming even more upset on the phone, her talk frantic and erratic.

'Francie, you've got to calm down, there's nothing you can do from where you are. Has anyone been around home?'

'What do you mean?'

'Has anyone talked to Mammy, have they searched the house or anything like that?' Dave was suddenly rational in his thinking. His first priority was to ensure that above all else his mother was safe. Stephen was a big boy who should be able to look after himself, but their mother was old and vulnerable. A common cold was a problem for Mammy, never mind the fears and complications of Stephen's predicament.

'No, not that I know of. I don't think they have any need to talk to her — like I said, they already know where you two are.'

'All right,' said Dave. 'You take it easy, go get a cup of tea and calm down. I'll find Stephen and warn him.

If need be, we'll head up to Dublin and get the next ferry to England. We'll not stay here, you've nothing to worry about.'

Francie seemed calmer then. 'Oh, please God you'll both be safe. Call me when you can.'

'I will. Love you, Francie.'

Dave hung up and walked out of the phone box. A flash of sunlight darted through a clearing in the otherwise overcast sky, but just as fast it vanished. Sirens screamed far off in the distance. Dave zipped up his overcoat. It felt like there was a storm on the way.

He knew he had to hurry, but he'd been seeing a woman for a few weeks and he must still meet her as planned. It would only be for a few minutes while he walked her home safely. At least he'd get to talk to her. If he and Stephen had to flee Ireland that night, he couldn't leave without an explanation. Dave quickened his pace.

March 1980

'Johnny, have you seen the girl Stephen's been going out with?'

Johnny sat reading the form guide on a quiet Saturday morning. A small bet here and there was one of the few luxuries he'd afforded himself over the years, and he'd developed a great fondness for the sport. What had begun as a simple wager one afternoon had soon become a hobby that Johnny took very seriously, dedicating his free time to the study of it.

'Luck is only a small factor when it comes to betting on horses: there's a lot of skill involved too,' he'd declared proudly to Stephen one day when they both had nothing better to do than to watch a race on television.

'Skill!' replied Stephen with a snigger. 'There's no skill involved. If there was then the bookies better watch out — you'd have them all out on their ears in no time.'

Johnny didn't flinch. 'You can laugh all you want, but it's true. Obviously there's a bit of luck involved: the track could be wet, the horse could be off form, the jockey might have been on the gargle the night before. But believe me, the rest of the time, if you study the sport and get to know the horses and their trainers, you can lower the risk.'

Despite his liking for the sport, Johnny didn't gamble that often, only when he was quite certain his odds were right. For the rest of the time, he'd read the form guide on a Saturday, mark out who he thought would win based on track histories of horses, jockeys and trainers, and then in the Sunday newspapers the following day, he'd check the results to see how he'd performed. He classed this ritual as training, and one thing was certain: it paid off. He may not have bet often but when he did he almost always struck a winner. One pound each way was his usual bet, which was conservative, given his success.

'So it's the usual again then, Johnny,' the betting clerk would say as he processed the wager.

'Yea, it's the usual.'

On one occasion, when Johnny's roll of success was particularly high, the betting clerk couldn't resist the urge to test him.

'I shouldn't say this, Johnny,' the clerk moved closer across the counter and lowered his voice, 'but if I were you, I would start increasing my bet. The good Lord knows that you hardly ever lose. You could win a fortune!'

Johnny smiled through his crooked teeth. 'No way, Mikey,' he replied, looking serious. 'My money is far too hard-earned for me to go squandering it on a bet. I promise you, the minute I get a bit cocky and start playing the bigger bets will be the exact time that I'll lose the lot.'

Mikey passed Johnny his slip and, later that afternoon, his winnings. 'Five pounds you won, Johnny. Can you imagine if you had bet your week's wages on that horse?'

'I can imagine it all right, but what kind of fool bets his week's wages?' He put the money in his pocket and left.

Johnny hadn't answered his question, so Dave came closer.

'Did you not hear me, Johnny? Do you know who the girl is that Stephen has been seeing? Are you deaf or something?' Dave pulled back the newspaper that Johnny held so close to his eyes. 'What's her name? Who is she?'

Johnny didn't answer. Instead he began nodding his

head in a teacher-like manner and making an aggravating *tut tut tut* sound.

'What's that supposed to mean?' Dave hated being mocked, and he knew exactly what Johnny was implying.

'Don't be getting jealous now, Dave,' he announced in a loud, over-the-top voice. 'It's not a crime for him to have a girlfriend, you know, it's not illegal down here in Southern Ireland.' Johnny began to laugh.

'I'm not fecking jealous, why would I care if he's seeing somebody or not?'

'You're jealous.' Johnny eyed Dave. 'I can see it written all over your face.'

'Would you ever cop on out of that!'

Johnny sat up in his seat. 'I'm not the smartest man on this planet but I can read you two boys like the boobs of a page three model. It's simple, you're the long termer and Stephen's the short!'

Dave was puzzled. 'What?' His voice increased in pitch. 'Long termer. What nonsense are you going on with?'

'You know what I mean, you go the long line with women while Stephen chops and changes on a weekly basis. You're the serious one and he's not.'

Johnny had struck a nerve with Dave. Why should this bother me? he thought. Who cares if Stephen has managed to get a girl so soon after arriving here in Stonebridge? Good on him! But no matter how Dave tried to sugar-coat it in his head, it did bother him. There were times, when they lived back in Belfast, that Dave wished he was more like his younger, less uptight brother. He had been in four long-term relationships over the years — all attributed by Stephen to his lack of conviction in breaking up with somebody.

'You've got to just tell her that you're not into her any more,' urged Stephen over a pint one evening when Dave's latest relationship had run its course.

'I've tried but she wants to give it one more go.' Dave sipped from his beer.

'Who cares if she wants to give it one more try; you're sick of her, you need to end it and find somebody new.'

'It's not as easy as that.' Dave was feeling a little awkward at receiving advice from his younger brother.

'That's what you said about your last two girlfriends and what happened with them? They ended up dumping you.' Stephen shook his head. 'I don't know how you get so serious with a girl; one minute you're kissing and the next you're talking about baby names. You're some fool. Do you want to know how I get rid of a woman?'

Dave smirked. 'I've a feeling you're going to tell me!'

'I fart!' said Stephen, laughing.

'You what?' The astonished look on Dave's face was priceless.

'That's how I get rid of a woman, I let off a fart in her company.'

Dave started to laugh. 'You're a headcase, do you know that?'

'I'm telling you the truth.' Stephen gulped the last of his pint and signalled the barman to bring two more. 'I'm too young to be tied down to just one girl, and so are you. I go out on a few dates, have a couple of laughs and when it feels like it's getting a bit serious, I let one fly.'

Dave laughed even louder. The casualness of Stephen's words was just too hilarious. He emptied the remainder of his beer and started on the newly poured one.

'These things are a bit too easy to drink,' he said as he wiped the froth from his lips, having downed a considerable mouthful.

'You're telling me.'

Johnny replied at last. 'Her name is June, the girl Stephen is seeing. June. Probably born then or something like that!'

Johnny had lost interest in chatting with Dave and returned his attention to the form guide. Dave stood thinking.

'The three thirty at the Curragh is a nice race, has a couple of good horses running, it could be a real winner.'

Dave despised horse racing, or gambling for that matter. He'd learnt that from his father, Noel. 'He was such a beautiful man,' Dave often commented about his father. 'A gentle soul with a huge heart. He would have given you the world if he had it, but he never did.' Noel was a stocky man, quite unlike his sons, who were each almost six feet tall. His face was long and narrow with a high forehead and he had comforting small eyes. Whenever Dave thought about his father, he always remembered the power that was in those eyes, the sheer strength and honesty. He was a good father, the kind that even other children liked to be in the company of, because of his joy in the limitless possibilities of youth.

'Dave, call mission control because we're about to take off into outer space,' he would say to his wide-eyed son, before taking a stool and flipping it upside down. 'This is your cockpit, get in!'

Dave loved playing games with his father; he never knew what to expect. He'd be sitting in between the four legs of the stool and Noel would commence the countdown: 'Ten — checking ignition; nine — booster rockets on; eight — checking the windscreen wipers are working —'

'Rockets don't have windscreen wipers,' Dave would say.

'Yes, they do,' Noel would answer. 'What if alien bugs get splattered on our windscreen by our laser guns — how will we get them off?' Dave beamed from ear to ear. 'Seven — turning on the navigational equipment ...'

Finally they would reach lift-off and Noel would mimic the sound that the rocket made, while pushing the youngster around the kitchen floor. They would whiz across the uneven surface, shooting imaginary laser beams at spaceships only they could see. Anne, Dave's mother, often struggled with her husband's antics, especially when he'd hype up the children not long before bedtime, all of them flying in separate spacecraft.

'Noel, stop all the playing around or they'll never sleep tonight,' she would shout during Noel's nightly playtime with his children. 'I don't know who is the bigger child, you or them.'

She would examine the stools for any damage and exclaim at the top of her lungs, 'You're lucky these chairs aren't broken or you'd be out in the shed tonight fixing them.' She always seemed to be annoyed with Noel for one thing or another but Dave never thought much of that, since most mothers he met seemed to be that way with their husbands. It was pretty typical that while fathers worked all day, mothers were masters of the house, and in Ireland you never put a foot wrong in Mammy's domain — child or husband.

Despite their squabbles, though, his parents were close and very happy together; Dave was always certain of that. In his childhood days public affection wasn't very common, even at home, and especially not around children. God forbid that it might corrupt their young minds. But Dave did manage to catch his parents exchanging moments with one another, a secretive kiss while the kids' backs were turned or an awkward leap away from each other when he entered the room unexpectedly. It was very rare but for Dave it was undeniable proof that, when the children were all fast asleep and his parents' guards were lowered, beneath the surface were two people who adored each other.

Dave loved memories of his parents like that: as simple as they were, they forged a truth in his mind which told him that beyond all else, the heart was the only thing that truly mattered. Perhaps it was because of their love for one another that Anne could cast a blind eye to Noel's flaw. There was never an argument or a harsh word spoken about this one real fault, the one thing that weakened beyond repair such a joyous, wholesome man. Maybe she loved him too much to accept that he might have a chink in his armour, and it was easier to pretend that it didn't exist at all. Fussing and fighting over play-acting with the children or not mowing the lawn or being home late from work was really inconsequential — that was what mothers did.

Afterwards, Dave often wondered if things could have been different.

As a child, Noel was undoubtedly Dave's hero, indestructible and flawless. But as the years went by, this image began to fade, though it wasn't until the evening of Dave's eighteenth birthday that he discovered his father's secret.

Dave was the only one at home when Noel stumbled in through the front door, barely standing, his face terribly bruised.

'Oh my God, what's happened to you?' Dave leapt up from his chair and raced to his father's aid.

'I'm okay, son,' Noel muttered, his breath coming in quick, whining gasps.

'You are in your eyes okay! Who did this to you?' Noel didn't answer; Dave eased the trembling man onto a seat before running to the kitchen for a wet cloth.

'Ah, thanks, son,' he said, biting his lip and stifling a moan as Dave wiped the blood from his face.

'Who did this, Dad, tell me, I'll call the police.'

'*No.*' Noel's eyes lit up, his voice was firm, and for the briefest of moments his pains became secondary.

'What do you mean, *no*? We have to call the police. Whoever did this to you might hurt someone else.'

Noel reached for his son's wrist and held it with wavering strength. 'No, son, we can't call the police, this was my own fault.'

Dave stared at his father blankly. 'What on earth did you do to deserve this kind of beating, Dad? You're in a mess, for Christ's sake.'

Noel clenched his teeth as another wave of pain came welling up. 'I can't tell you, Dave. I can't.'

'Mammy's going to be home soon, what will we tell her when she finds you looking like this?' Dave examined the injuries a little more closely. As he wiped away the blood from his dad's face he could see three definite gashes across the cheeks. 'It's really bad. You poor sod, it must have been terrible. You might need to see a doctor.'

Only much later would Noel be able to tell him about the man with the iron bar. How he'd seemed to pounce from out of nowhere and deliver the first blow to his face before Noel realised what was happening.

Then he was on the ground trying to defend himself against the second assault, which landed with great force against his nose, sending blood in all directions. And then came the blows to the body.

For now, Noel faced his son. 'I'm a gambler, Davie, I have been for years.'

'A gambler?' Dave was genuinely surprised. 'Since when? I've never once seen you gamble.'

'I'm a gambler, Dave.'

'No, you're not,' persisted Dave. 'In the eighteen years that I've been alive, I've never heard you once mention the word *gamble*, let alone seen you put on a bet.'

Noel rose from his chair and examined his injuries in the mirror. His face was swollen and unfamiliar. He turned slowly to face his son again. 'Davie, it's true. I've kept it a secret for all these years, but — you need to know, I gamble a lot.' Noel paused. 'I've had my highs and my lows. There's been days when you just couldn't stop me, no matter what I put money on, it came in a winner. But lately I haven't been having many of those days, lately I'm just chasing the next win and it's getting further and further away. It's a vicious circle. I borrowed money to try to win back the money I'd lost, and when that didn't work I borrowed some more ... Davie, these people I borrowed from, they're as rough as you'll ever meet and I owe them a lot of money.'

Dave was stunned, and struggling. Standing before him, battered and bruised, scared and unsure, was his *father*, his hero. Dave usually confided in him, it was normally Dave who needed support and encouragement and strength, not his father.

'Dad,' he said softly, 'how could you keep this from us all these years, without any of us ever suspecting something?' Then he began to see. To correlate his recollections, to think of all those facets of his life where his father's addiction must have placed its hand. He suddenly remembered a time when he was ten years old and meals were reduced to bread and porridge. His mind drifted then to a Christmas morning when his mother explained to all the children how Santa had been delayed on the way from the North Pole and that their presents would arrive in January.

A mass of thoughts flooded Dave's head now, thoughts of fluctuating fortunes, times when money was plentiful but, more often than not, times when it was scarce. How often had Mammy summoned all the kids into the living room with fury painted across her face and the money jar in one hand? 'Who took from the money jar?' she would yell, waving it in all their faces. The money jar, which sat in the glass cabinet beside the fireplace, was a small porcelain sugar bowl. Noel's wages went into the money jar, the change from the weekly shopping went into the jar. That money jar was the family vault — but, thinking back, Dave remembered too many occasions when its security was compromised. Money was forever disappearing.

'It's a sin to steal and especially from your own family. If nobody admits to taking the money this second, you'll all go to bed without any dinner!' She would eye each one of the children and, on hearing no confession, she would stay true to her warning. 'Off to bed, the lot of you, go, out of my sight.'

Dave remembered how the children would leave the room, blaming each other for not telling the truth, for their unfair punishment. He remembered the bitterness it created between them. Now, as eighteen-year-old Dave stood before Noel, having heard his father's confession, he suddenly realised the impact this secret had had on the family over the years.

'You should be ashamed of yourself, Dad.' He was upset now, his temples pounded thickly and his throat was tight.

'I'm sorry, Davie, I —'

'Don't give me that,' Dave interrupted sharply. 'I remember now — the money jar — and all the time it was you. Was it because of you that our car suddenly vanished one day, or that we went for weeks one time eating the same food day and night because Mam said we had to tighten our belts? Was that all you? Are you the reason why Mam had to sell her jewellery? I remember it all now.'

'I'm sorry, Davie, honestly, what can I say, I'm sorry! We've all got our demons Davie, every one of us.'

'Not me,' exclaimed Dave, strong now and direct. 'Not me. I would never do to my family what you've done to us.'

'You don't know that, Davie — you'd be surprised what can happen,' Noel said bitterly.

'No way, I wouldn't be stupid enough. Who *are* you?' he continued with greater clarity. 'You're not the man I've been looking up to all of my life. You're somebody else, somebody who keeps secrets and treats his family badly.'

'I'm not, Davie, please don't talk to me like that.' He swayed as though he'd taken a blow to the head.

'To be honest, I can't talk to you at all right now. I barely want to look at you.' The words came from his mouth involuntarily, they were spoken before he realised their spite.

Noel was grey-faced. 'Davie, I'm really hurt, I need

your help. They've only given me until six tonight to pay up! They said they'll kill me.'

Dave pressed his temples with his fingers, his mind racing. He needed to collect himself. Finally he chose not to speak, but to leave the room.

'Where are you going?' cried Noel. 'Don't leave me, Davie, please, I need your help. *Davie.*'

Dave slammed the front door behind him and began to march through the bleak streets of Andersonstown. It was a rare, brilliant blue day, but it may as well have been cloudy — he had been rained upon and he needed to shake off the wet. He hadn't left for good, just for long enough to let things settle in his mind and to make his father understand how angry he was. The Republic Bar, about five minutes up the road, caught his eye and he thought it would be a good place to defuse.

'One pint of lager,' he called out to the barman as he entered the quiet pub.

Unlike most of his friends, Dave had never touched an alcoholic drink before and, while he waited for the pint to be poured, he felt a degree of anticipation of that first sip. But when it arrived in front of him Dave took very little time to savour the taste, downing it in a matter of minutes. It felt good. With each mouthful his heartbeat slowed down a bit more. His mind started to relax and he was beginning to feel like he could face his father again.

'Another one,' he called out to the old barman in the crumpled black suit. One glass didn't feel quite enough.

Having finished his second pint, drinking less quickly than before, Dave decided that it was time to return home and deal with his father.

'It's not like he's a murderer,' remarked Dave aloud as he walked, suddenly remorseful. There's worse things he could have done, he thought. Clarity was being restored and his father was returning to his pedestal, perhaps not as high as it used to be but a pedestal all the same. Dave glanced at his watch: it was five to six. The loan shark would be arriving at his home any minute.

'Shit!' Dread began to course through his veins and he started to run.

He saw images of his father lying face down in the living room, his life cut short to settle a bad debt. He could see his mam arriving home from her sister's with Stephen and Francie close behind. Then he could see himself, trying to understand why he hadn't been there for his father when he needed him most.

'If I had known it was so late!' he panted, turning the corner. His house was fourth in a row of ten. As he neared it, everything looked fine: young girls still played hopscotch on the street, Mickey O'Carroll the coal man was delivering fuel two doors up and the blue sky of summer was still blue. Dave was breathless from running when he reached the front door. But there he stopped abruptly.

The door was already open — and inside he could hear a voice. An unfamiliar male voice.

Fuck, Dave thought, his heart thumping out of his skin.

His immediate thought was to stall — listen at the door and formulate a plan — but he knew there was no time for that. With an almighty thrust, he threw the front door wider and stormed inside, along the hallway and into the living room.

The first thing he saw was a curled-up heap on the floor. His father.

Standing over Noel was a man with a knife. He turned to face Dave, and with this movement came a clearer sight of Noel — writhing in pain but still alive.

'Son, don't you get involved in this,' warned the loan shark in a thick gravelly voice. He was shorter and older than Dave had imagined, but there was a dangerous air about him, and his eyes appeared black and lifeless. Strangely, he also looked no different from anyone you might meet on the street.

Dave's eyes were drawn to the knife the man held firmly in his left hand.

'Your father was given a warning and he didn't listen. You best get on your way.'

Powering forward, Dave charged the man with the knife, catching him off guard. Somehow Dave's head met with the other man's forehead, and the painful smack sent both of them tumbling to the floor and the knife sliding some place out of reach. Dave struggled to rise, his head pounding from the impact. But the loan shark recovered quicker. He turned to face Dave, his jaw and fists tight, and delivered his first punch, then another and another. Young and still slender, Dave didn't stand a chance.

He was hurled back onto the floor, crashing like a dead weight. Pain needled into him in quick hard bursts. His body felt insubstantial.

As he lay on the floor, Dave's eyes met his father's; both men were spent. Above them, the loan shark towered.

Dave felt something at the tips of his fingers, something solid, something made of wood. He had no idea what it was and he hadn't the strength to look around at the object. The man above them stood motionless for a second; he seemed to be thinking about what he should do. Then, he reached into his coat pocket and brought out a knuckle-duster.

Dave thought, this isn't how I go out.

The shark looked briefly behind him then placed the iron weapon across his knuckles.

'*No!*' Dave suddenly roused himself.

He stretched out his hand and grabbed the object. With a swift relentless move he drove his arm into the air. Unknowingly, he'd found the knife.

To the assailant's horror, the knife had caught his wrist, and Dave slammed him down to the floor. The loan shark let out a violent roar — but Dave, seeing what was happening, felt a raw and vicious impulse to go harder. Holding firm to the knife, he continued to drive it further into the loan shark's wrist, staking his arm the wooden floor.

'Fuck!' screamed the man. But Dave knew that he couldn't stop there.

He had to finish things off. With his right hand, he maintained pressure on the knife that was holding the loan shark in place, while with his left he began to thump and thrash his face. Blood spilled everywhere as Dave hammered the man with his fist, slamming his head to one side. The loan shark tried to fight back, but he'd been caught in a corner.

Now the fight came swiftly to an end. And a new fear set in.

Dave sat back away from the limp body of the loan shark, and turned to his father, who was beginning to lift himself up off the floor.

'There was nothing else I could do!' Tears fell down Dave's face. 'You saw it, there was nothing I could do.'

Both men sat in shock.

'Is he dead?' Noel finally asked in a low, desperate voice.

'I don't know.' wept Dave, 'I think so.'

'Check if he is.'

Dave approached the loan shark one more time, and placed a hand on the man's chest. Immediately he leapt back in horror and joy.

'He's alive,' he yelled, and with that came some movement from the man.

'Finish him off,' shouted Noel.

'I *can't*.'

The man opened his bloodied eyes but remained still. Seconds later he began to move his head, and tried to rise to his feet. Dave and Noel watched, appalled, as he pulled the knife from the floorboard it was wedged in, freeing his wrist, and stood up. Nobody, including the man, seemed to know what should happen next.

Dave faced the loan shark as he rose. They stood eye to eye but neither spoke. Then Dave saw defeat in the man's eyes and it was clear that the fight was over. Moments later the loan shark turned away and left the house.

'No one can know about this,' said Noel at once.

'No one will,' replied Dave.

As quickly as he could manage, Dave scrubbed the floor and removed all evidence of what had happened. Meanwhile, Noel left the house and caught a train for county Tyrone; the excuse would be his sick mother.

When Anne arrived home, there was only Dave to see. 'Oh, Jesus, Mary and Joseph, what happened to your face?' she cried.

'Stop fussing, Mammy,' declared Dave, 'it's the other fellow you should be worried about, not me.'

And though the days that followed were, for Dave, mainly spent looking fearfully over his shoulder, Noel eventually paid his bad debt, and the loan shark never returned.

'Morning!' Years later in Stonebridge, on the Sunday two weeks before Francie's call to Dave, Stephen entered the kitchen barely awake, dressed shabbily in shapeless white pyjamas, his hair ruffled, his voice husky. 'What a night,' he moaned a little queasily, scratching his head and trying to decide whether to have cereal or to boil the kettle.

'You're telling me,' agreed Dave. 'My head feels like it's been run under a train.'

Johnny sniggered from his armchair. As usual, he had paced last night's drinking better than they had.

'You guys were downing those pints like they were going out of fashion. Especially you, Dave.'

Shame pulsed through Dave and he couldn't let the moment pass without asking, 'Did I make an ass of myself?'

Johnny shrugged off the question. 'Do you not remember?'

'No, I don't. What did I do?'

'Ah, Dave, stop having us on,' Stephen said jovially as he filled up the kettle, 'you couldn't have been that drunk, sure we left the pub earlier than normal.'

'Yea, because we were *told* to leave,' interrupted Johnny, rising from his chair.

'Aha!' Dave looked at Johnny. 'You're pissed off with me and that's why you've hardly talked to me all morning.'

'I'm not pissed off. I've hardly talked to you because the only thing you want to chat about is your brother's new girlfriend.'

Stephen's ears pricked up. 'I knew it would get the better of you sooner or later.'

'Never mind that,' continued Dave, a little anxious. 'So what did I do that was so bad last night?'

He knew he wasn't an angry drunk — well, at least he always hoped as much. Generally he would become more boisterous with drink, the leader of the party; he was the one who always tried to keep things going.

'You don't know when you've had enough!' his sister Francie had once remarked, to which Dave had replied, 'You don't know when to have fun.'

Stephen opened the back door, inviting a rush of cold morning air into the kitchen. 'Sorry, guys, I've got to get this off my chest —' The bitter chill invaded the room as Stephen stood barefoot on the door ledge, coughing hard and spitting out the phlegm from his throat.

'That's disgusting!' exclaimed Johnny.

Dave agreed, and Stephen shut the door and turned to him.

'You started pinching everybody's arse.'

Dave was astonished and slightly amused. 'Who, me?'

'Yea,' Johnny cut in, 'you, Dave. You went around the bar pinching the arse of everybody you met. It was embarrassing.'

Dave wasn't convinced. 'You guys are having me on, I didn't do that.'

'Did you what?' Stephen livened up. 'I looked over to you at one point and you were chatting away to some bloke while, at the same time, grabbing the cheeks of a good-looking girl who was standing behind you.'

Dave's eyes opened wide with surprise.

'You made a show of yourself, Dave.' Johnny wasn't impressed, but Stephen found it very amusing.

'Don't worry, Dave,' he said with an easy smile, 'you only pissed off a few people, everybody else thought it was a good laugh.' Stephen tipped a spoonful of coffee into a mug and began to fill it with hot water.

Dave continued to look bewildered. 'You know, I can't remember doing anything like that. The last thing I remember is talking with you, Stephen, about this June of yours. Johnny's just told me that's her name.'

'I told you her name last night, you idiot.'

'I don't remember that either — but anyway, where was your June last night? Did she turn up?'

Stephen shook his head and sipped from his coffee. 'No, but she told me up front that she mightn't be able to make it, something about her father being a bit on the strict side.'

Dave scoffed. 'How old is this girl, ten?'

'Don't mind him, Stephen,' interrupted Johnny. 'Dave's a bit jealous, he can't understand how you've scored and he hasn't.'

Dave threw Johnny a filthy look. 'I'm not fucking jealous, I'm just interested in hearing a bit about her. What's she like? Has she got a sister?'

'She does.' Stephen perked up again. 'Susan. And you know what, how about I arrange a double date, two brothers with two sisters?'

His eyes gleamed with enthusiasm, but now Dave wasn't so sure.

'What's she like, this sister?'

'She's great, don't worry — and anyway, beggars can't be choosers. I'll see if I can arrange something with June for tonight.'

'All right, but Susan better be good-looking,' replied Dave with little to no enthusiasm. But later he thought, What have I got to lose?

June
&
Mattie

'Button up that jacket, Mattie, it's freezing!'

Mattie didn't seem to notice the cold in the same way that others did. He couldn't understand what all the fuss was about. It was definitely cold but not nearly as cold as it was up in Iceland or in the Antarctic with the penguins and the explorers.

'This isn't Iceland.' She'd read his mind. 'And anyway, in Iceland the Eskimos rug up ten times more than we do here in Ireland. You'll thank me when you don't get a cold this winter!'

Mattie shrugged. A mist of fog rolled from his mouth as he sighed and for a moment it kept him amused as he pretended to be a train puffing smoke from its smokestack.

'You still haven't buttoned up your coat.'

'But I'm hot,' he whined. 'I don't want to!'

'Just do what you're told!' Her tone went from soft to stern effortlessly; she had authority in her voice, a firm control that comes from experience. Mattie knew he was crossing the boundary of her patience and finally did as he was instructed.

'That's a good boy!'

'Yea but I'm still hot,' he grumbled under his breath.

Two girls caught Mattie's eye. They'd been walking on the path opposite to him.

'He's so weird,' one could be heard saying.

'Yea, he's the weirdest kid in the school, I think!'

They continued to stare and chat, maintaining a close distance and giggling intermittently. Mattie was tired of it.

'Shut your mouths, you slags!' he spoke quickly and with venom. 'I'm not deaf, you know, I can hear your big fat mouths, you fatarses!'

The girls were dumbfounded.

'You're a freak and everyone knows it,' said one of them.

'At least I don't smell!' returned Mattie.

The girls threw their noses in the air and scurried off up ahead, grumbling as they fled. 'The cheek of him!'; 'Fatarses?' Their voices faded as they drifted out of earshot.

'Mattie, that was very rude and you know it.' She too was dumbfounded.

'No it wasn't,' he grumbled. 'Those girls were making fun of me and having a good laugh.'

'Does that give you the right to call them names?'

'Yes it does. They'd no right to be talking about me!'

'Did it ever occur to you that one of them might have fancied you; girls sometimes do that, you know!'

'No, Mam!' The whine made it clear how absurd he thought her comment was.

'Either way, you should feel very guilty for speaking like that: it was very rude!'

Mattie frowned. 'Sorry!' he mumbled.

The walk from his house to the tired stale walls of the Holy Mary Primary School was a brisk fifteen minutes. The roads were icy, the trees were stripped bare of colour and the sky was a continuously dull depressing grey. Occasionally Mattie would step off the footpath to pound his foot into puddles that had frozen over during the night's frost or to take a chance sliding along short stretches of iced-over road. June watched with amusement; he always had to be busy with something.

'We nearly lived in one of those houses,' sighed his mother as they passed by yet another estate, one of the more up-market and respectable ones.

'I know,' replied Mattie distantly. A car suddenly whizzed by, startling him back onto the footpath.

'You've got to be careful, Mattie, some people around here have no sense!' The car disappeared around a bend, scaring other kids along the way.

There was no scenery throughout the short journey to school, just housing estate after housing estate, each with its own story. Some looked better than others. Some, like the one Mattie lived in, had crumbled under the strife.

'Nearly there,' Mattie announced, seeing the school up ahead.

'Where's Niall today?' asked his mother.

'I don't know. Maybe his dad drove him.' Mattie looked away.

'Really?' said June. 'He hasn't met you in the morning for a while now, has he?'

'No,' frowned Mattie. The truth came out in a rush. 'He said his dad didn't want him to walk with me any more!'

'Why not?'

'I don't know. I can still go over theirs.' Mattie shrugged. 'It's not because of me, his dad just doesn't like him walking to school. Anyway, he knows I'm with you in the mornings.'

June pondered his response for a second. 'How are things with you and Susan?'

'All right, I suppose.' Mattie crashed his foot into a frozen puddle, breaking the ice and sending filthy water spraying everywhere.

'Be careful, Mattie!' scolded his mother. 'Look at your trousers, you're a state now to be walking into your classroom.'

'Sorry.' He was less convincing this time.

June shook her head then stopped and faced her son. 'Mattie, you've got to be the best that you can be; once you start letting yourself down, you let down your whole family too. You're not a little boy any more, you're a young man. You have to be good for Aunty Susan. I know she's mad about you seeing me but that doesn't give you any right to be bold. She loves you and whatever feelings she has towards me have nothing to do with you.

'Okay, Mam.' Mattie eyed the zebra crossing up ahead and, wishing to put an end to the conversation, suggested they get on before he was late for school. Terry Byrne the lollipop man met him at the crossing.

'Good morning, Mattie!' declared Terry with a huge grin across his flushed round face. 'No dynamic duo today, eh, no sign of young Niall?'

Mattie laughed. 'Ah it doesn't matter, I've got Mam here instead.'

'Ah yes, of course, much better,' he nodded. 'Sorry, June, your boy is getting so tall that I hardly saw you behind him there. You'd better hurry on in,' he said to Mattie, 'or you'll be late.'

'All right,' yawned Mattie and then, turning to his mam, 'will you be meeting me after school today?'

'Ah I won't be able to, Mattie; anyway, you need to get home fast, your dad is coming back. Don't be late.'

Mattie was off already. 'See you later!' he yelled as he hurried through the school gates, stopping just once to look back and wave goodbye to his mother. June had already left.

Seeing Dave in an English police cell was beyond anything June could handle. 'Dave, I'm finished with all of this.' She pressed her fingers against her temples. 'I'm that stressed my head feels like it's going to explode. How many times have I begged you to quit? You can't handle it, you never could. And now look at the state of you, locked up in a gaol cell. *Drink-driving*, Dave? You could have killed someone.' June looked away briefly. 'And the more shame me for sticking by you all this time when the only one who really matters is Mattie.' She faced him again. 'I'm sick, Dave, sick from all of this, and I don't have the strength any more.'

'Catch yourself on, June,' he'd slurred in his thick Belfast accent, grappling with the iron bars of the cell to help himself to stand upright. 'What are you going on with. Will you just get me out of here, for Christ's sake?'

'No, Dave, this time you're on your own.'

'*June*,' he yelled, rousing the night officer on charge, 'get me the fuck out of here!'

June was filled with horror and disappointment. 'Forget it. Goodbye, Dave!' And she turned and headed for the door.

'June! June! For the love of God, June, help me out!' Dave's voice continued to echo as the officer shut the door behind her and June suddenly found herself alone in the parking lot.

She contained her tears until she was back in the car, where she sat for forty minutes unable to start the engine. The streets were still, shrouded in a layer of orange neon lighting. It was past midnight, Monday, and most people were already fast asleep. Why couldn't Dave have been too? Why had they even bothered with 'a new life' in England? Nothing new except the street names, she thought. Same small-town life, same on-and-off work, same drinking.

Finally, she drove back to the house to pack.

And then poor Mattie kept on at her about why they had to leave so suddenly, and why his daddy wasn't coming with them.

'Will he be meeting us at the boat?' the boy asked as they sat together on the bus journey to the dock.

'No.'

'Why not?'

'Because he won't,' she snapped, and then immediately softened her tone. 'Mattie, please, no more questions, I'll explain everything when the time is right.'

'Okay, Mammy.'

The truth was that she didn't have any answers for him, none that were concrete, at least. I'm still figuring this out for myself, she thought soberly, and then asked herself the same questions she'd been asking all afternoon: Have I done the right thing? And what's going to happen to Dave?

There had been so many times over the years when she thought that she might leave Dave and on each occasion she'd imagined the happiness that she would feel at the release. Now that it had finally happened, she felt no happiness whatsoever. There was a void where her heart used to be.

'But he isn't a bad man,' she whispered to herself as she stood on the deck of the ferry, gazing across the water while drizzling rain fell upon her uncovered head. To those watching from inside, she resembled an ill-fated lover from some Hollywood movie. Alone on deck, her slender figure still, she looked off into the distance, distracted from the chaotic world around her, consumed by thoughts. Mattie could see her too. Even drenched by the rain, June was beautiful, her features soft against the harsh conditions of the Irish Sea.

He's a great man, she thought. I'm such a cold bitch! The ferry dipped, slamming into turbulent waves and sending whitewash in every direction. No, I'm *not* a bitch. I was *always* there for him and he let me down time and time again.

'Missus, you really should come inside, for your own safety!'

June disregarded the warning from the bearded gentleman in the blue rain jacket and turned away as he fled back indoors. The ferry rocked from side to side and June tried to maintain her balance.

Her hands clung tightly to the iron railings, icy cold and slippery wet. She could not escape the good thoughts of Dave, thoughts of happier times, the memories of her husband on days when his demons didn't drive him towards drink. She wanted to think of the booze-fuelled arguments instead, the slamming doors and the embarrassing displays of drunkenness, but she couldn't.

Well, it makes no difference now, she thought, I can't go back to England.

Mattie was in the enclosed deck of the boat and from where June stood she could see that he was content, reading his comic book. Did he have any comprehension of what was going on? He must, thought June, he sees everthing.

She smiled. It was sometimes hard to remember Mattie as a baby, dependent and so small. Those days were exciting, she thought, we hadn't a clue what we were doing but we managed all the same.

'I've got the technique down pat,' Dave had whispered to her one day as he rocked baby Mattie, who was snuggled fast asleep in his arms. 'It's all in the movement.'

June regarded her husband with amusement as he waltzed slowly in a circle, lifting and lowering his body as he moved.

'You'll have to teach me that some time,' she'd said with a smirk.

It was mid-June, not long after Mattie was born, and his parents were coming to terms with this new and challenging chapter of their lives. Nappies and breastfeeding, sleepless nights and utter confusion.

'I wouldn't trade it for the world,' Dave had declared, his eyes glowing with pride. 'And as for you,' he approached June and knelt down to where she lay in the bed. 'You are the most gorgeous wee lassie I have ever set my eyes on.' June tried to conceal her blushes; she had never been one for compliments.

'Look at this little guy,' Dave continued, overwhelmed by the bundle in his arms. 'You made him, you and your gorgeous body and your,' he thought for a second, 'your super strength.'

'Super strength?' June raised an inquisitive eyebrow. 'I'm glad you didn't say where!'

'Of course I wouldn't say that,' he replied with a sly smile. 'It's because of your super strength that you could endure that pain. And I'm not saying where *that* was, either! My God, you're Superwoman, for Christ's sakes.'

June lay back on her propped-up pillows, admiring the two men in her life. 'Look at *you*,' she mused. 'I think this is the happiest I've ever seen you.'

'I think it might well be the happiest I've felt, I just can't get over it. June is definitely a lucky month for me.'

Mattie moved in his arms and both parents looked at each other with the same thought — it was great that he was asleep but it wouldn't be such a bad thing if he woke up. He didn't though, he just continued to wriggle a little more and then relaxed back in his deep sleep.

'It's just so hard to believe that we're parents.' Dave spoke with a sense of wonder, the grandness and the complexity of their new responsibilities still unfolding for him.

'Do you think we'll be good parents?' asked June, a hint of nervousness in her voice.

'Of course,' answered Dave with absolute confidence. 'I'll tell you one thing: this wee man I'm holding in my arms doesn't have a clue about how good he already has it. There's nothing in this world that we won't do to make sure Mattie has the best life possible.'

'I know that, but that wouldn't make us good parents, it would just make us good providers. What about teaching him right from wrong and helping him with his homework? What about being able to recognise when he's got things on his mind, or if he's in trouble — will we be good at all that?'

'One second,' instructed Dave, 'let me put him back to bed.'

Dave carefully lowered Mattie into his basket and, unable to resist the temptation, kissed him on the forehead.

'Goodnight, little guy, love you.' Then he climbed into bed beside June and invited her to rest on his arm, which she did lovingly.

'Don't worry, June,' he said. 'I know it won't be easy and I'd be lying if I said we'd get everything right along the way, but one thing is for sure, you and I have seen enough in our lives to know what's the best way for *us* to teach *our* boy. Everything will be fine.'

June was silent and Dave knew she wasn't content with his answer.

'*And*,' he continued, 'you will be the best mother a boy could ever hope for. You've got a heart of gold and you're the smartest person I've ever known. There's nothing that you won't be able to do for Mattie, nothing.'

June smiled and nestled into his embrace; she had heard what she needed to hear. 'We better get some sleep, it's almost three o'clock,' she yawned.

'You're right. I'm wrecked and I've a long day tomorrow. Goodnight, love.'

She remembered all this now, riding the Irish Sea as the waves rose to unnerving heights, crashing at the hull of the ferry. White spray cascaded down over the deck. For a brief moment June lost her footing and slid — but she kept her firm grasp on the ferry railings. It was a ridiculous martyrdom for her to risk being on this deck; the unseasonal weather was barely suitable for the ferry crossing, let alone for a woman on some kind of masochistic trip.

She had managed to remain calm up until the ferry boarded, so much in control of her actions that it had briefly felt easier than she had expected to leave him.

Even Mattie, after the initial shock had subsided, appeared quite accepting of their sudden journey. But as she'd stepped on board the over-crowded ferry, her eyes had met those of other passengers: some were excited but for the most part there was a tiredness to everyone, a sense of the habitual. And she'd felt the reality of her circumstances come crashing in on her.

She would have to face family and friends back in Ireland; people who would console her, people who would look down on her and, worse yet, people who would tell her that they'd warned her from the start to stay away from such a man as Dave — people like her own father. She'd have to move back into the council house that Dave hated so much, and which they'd left in Susan's hands.

There was no easy solution — whatever way she ran through it in her mind, she was still a woman who'd taken flight away from her husband — and she knew too well that the wagging tongues of the local community enjoyed keeping stories like this alive.

Terry Byrne came to mind, the lollipop man, a wild scoundrel who'd slept with his brother's wife and mocked the church. Though her story wasn't that kind of scandal, she was still reminded of how long people had talked about Terry, how his story never ceased to amuse, years after it took place.

'What a ridiculous thing to be thinking,' she mumbled gruffly, wiping her saturated hair from her face. She was freezing cold out here on the deck, but still she was unbending.

Dave rose to mind again. She remembered one summer day at a time of year when the long bright evenings freed Ireland from its seemingly unending greyness, quite unlike today. When she thought of summer she thought of the simple things: the smell of a freshly mown lawn; the hush of a gentle breeze in the countryside where a quiet laneway made for a lovers' retreat; the abundance of colours that presented themselves in almost every direction. Summer was Ireland's only refuge each year from the battle with the elements and June loved it more than any other time.

That day Dave had placed his hands over June's eyes. 'You have to keep them closed until we're there.'

It wasn't much further. They had already been walking in sparse forest for about five minutes, careful on the uneven ground, but Dave knew that his intended destination was just up ahead.

'Where are we going?' June laughed.

'You'll see,' replied Dave.

June was very pregnant with Mattie. Dave had planned the afternoon for some time, trying to make sure that everything was just right and that June didn't have an inkling of what was in store.

'All right, sweetheart, open your eyes!'

He removed his hands, and June caught her first glimpse of the surprise he'd prepared for her.

All around them towered lush evergreen trees, swaying ever so slightly, standing like protectors over the forest. Blades of sunlight cut through the thick canopy of green, casting welcome warmth and light, while at their feet was a bed of thick clover, green and vibrant like a newly laid carpet. Up ahead, between four huge trees, was a white blanket, spread neatly as far as it could stretch. On its surface was a bottle of wine, two glasses and a small basket of food.

'I don't believe it,' she spoke slowly. 'A picnic?'

Dave grinned like a rewarded child. 'Well, I figured you deserved a nice little surprise before you pop.' Dave placed a hand on June's stomach. 'I think the little one knows what's going on. She — he — is running around in there.'

June was still amazed. 'I think he or she is running around because we can't believe you actually made a picnic. You hate picnics!'

Dave had gestured with his hands and shoulders like a Mafia boss. 'What can I say, it's the least I can do!'

June smiled now, recalling that day and that gesture. But the rain began to fall more heavily on the deck, and she finally decided to retreat into the enclosed area.

Why did that picnic mean so much to me? she thought. It was such a simple surprise on the surface, but deeply embedded in the ham sandwiches, chopped apples and white wine was the essence of her man. He was the one who knew her better than anyone else, he was a man who made promises and kept them and he was a man who would sacrifice anything for his family. She had mentioned her love for picnics when they first started dating and he had told her how much he disliked outings like that. 'But I'll bring you on one, mark my words.' He'd wagged his finger. 'One day when you don't expect it I'm going to bring you to a little spot in a forest and treat you to the best picnic of your life!'

It might have been over a year later, but he was true to his word.

'Mammy, you're soaking wet!' Mattie tilted his head disapprovingly as June came in from the dreadful weather. So then she expected people to stare, to look at her as a reckless mother who had some kind of death wish. But everyone was too involved in their own thoughts, in their own journeys. No one had any interest in a woman who was just now leaving her husband — the same husband who, for some reason, she could no longer blame or resent.

'When we get to Ireland, will Grandad be picking us up?'

June grimaced at the thought of her father's long, stern face greeting her on their arrival. 'I hope not,' she said, scowling.

'What?' Mattie was staring. She hadn't meant to sound so negative.

'I —' She thought for a second. 'I hope not, because it's a long drive for Grandad and he's quite old now.' Whatever differences she had with her father, whatever irreparable damage he had caused to her or Dave over the years, she never wanted Mattie to see his grandfather in a bad light.

Mattie scratched his head. Something wasn't right.

'You don't like Grandad any more, Mammy, do you?'

His words reminded her of something Dave had once said about their son, when he was only two years of age. 'You know what,' he'd remarked, watching Mattie play with toy bricks. 'That boy hears and understands everything you and I are saying. He doesn't miss a thing.'

Did she still love her father? It wasn't an easy question to answer any more. So much had passed between them. So much hurt. We should never have lived at home, she thought, and her mind wandered back to that caravan, raised on concrete bricks in the back garden of her parents' home.

It wasn't what Dave or June had hoped for, but it had been better than nothing.

'We can't live in a caravan,' Dave had protested at the time. 'And especially not in your parents' backyard!'

When June's parents offered her their caravan it was solely for her and Mattie's sake — as far as they were concerned, Dave could sleep on the street. His job as husband had been to provide and when he didn't do that — and had instead signed himself on for the dole, much to his own disappointment and after several weeks of looking for work — June's parents had snubbed him.

'Jesus, June,' Dave yelled one evening in the hollow caravan, 'you know they're treating me like shite, why won't you say something? Your father talks to me like I'm a second-class citizen. I've never felt so useless in all my life.'

'No, he doesn't — and anyway, what do you want me to say to them? They're my parents, for God's sake. I know it's not the Ritz here, but without this caravan we'd be out on the streets.'

June had used the out-on-the-streets argument before and Dave despised it. 'You're saying we owe them! Are you joking me? We've hit tough times financially and they're in a position to help us, I think as parents it's their duty. I know I'd do it for Mattie without question. And, June, please stop talking about living on the streets, I hate it — you know I would never let that happen.'

June had said nothing. Dave needed to soften his tone if he was going to reason with her.

'Look, all I'm asking is that you stand up for me. You could at least do that.'

'Stand *up* for you!' June was suddenly angry, and confused. 'Stand up for what?'

This was harsh and Dave had to take a moment to contain himself. A dull silence fell; the whole van seemed upset. Finally Dave spoke, in a soft, disappointed tone.

'Nothing I ever do will be enough for you, will it? You love me when things are easy but the minute times get difficult you turn the other way. You know damn well that I'm not just another lazy prick, I'll do anything and ... I do everything for you and for Mattie.'

Dave looked hard-faced at June for a moment before hurling himself out of the caravan, slamming the tin door as he left.

Tears had welled in June's eyes. She'd tried to busy herself by tidying up, but she couldn't believe she'd been so hurtful. Finally she resigned herself to getting into bed and crying into her pillow.

It was true that Michael, June's father, had disliked Dave from the beginning. Absurdly, it was his accent. Her father had always said, 'I haven't met a Northern Irish man that I've liked. They're the reason this country's in a mess.' When he discovered that his daughter had fallen for just such a man, he was appalled.

'No daughter of mine is going to marry a northerner,' he had roared the evening he heard the news of her engagement. 'He didn't even have the decency to ask me first.'

'He told me that he tried,' replied June defensively. 'But you wouldn't speak to him, you wouldn't even let him talk.'

'That's nonsense. He's a liar, he never came anywhere near me.' June fell silent and Michael knew he'd struck a nerve. 'You can't trust him, June. If he can lie to you about this then what else will he lie to you about? If you go ahead with this wedding, you will have let me down.'

June left the room disheartened. Her father had shamelessly planted a seed in her mind. That evening she asked, 'Dave, did you really try to meet with my dad to ask if you could marry me?'

'Of course I did,' he replied coldly, 'but the fool wouldn't give me the time of day.'

'Don't call him a fool.'

Dave looked at June sharply. 'Why do you ask?'

'Dad said —' June began, but stopped.

'"*Dad* said?" Said what? That I never tried to talk to him?'

Dave stared at her, and then stepped back in disbelief. 'And you don't know who to believe! Come on, June, he's messing with your head and he's loving it.'

June hesitated before speaking again. 'So, *you're* telling the truth?'

Dave smiled sadly. 'Have I ever lied to you before? I don't know what it is about your father but when it comes to him, you and Susan are like putty. He must be a real sergeant major.'

June frowned but didn't answer.

Michael's opinion of Dave had never changed and even on their wedding day he found an excuse not to attend the party. June had felt dreadful and Dave was livid. 'He's an absolute prick,' he'd said to his sister Francie. 'The only one he cares about is himself.'

Dave hated living in the caravan, and thought Michael must love being able to spy on them night and day.

'I hear you've lost your job,' Michael had said in a stern monotone on the very evening of Dave's unemployment. 'You didn't last long, did you?'

'Michael, I wasn't the only one that was let go, it's not like I did something wrong. There're cutbacks everywhere, hundreds of people are out looking for work.'

Michael scowled. 'Don't make pathetic excuses.'

Dave shrank.

'I realise,' continued Michael, 'that for young men these days, responsibility isn't as high on the agenda as it was in mine.' There were so many things Dave could have said but he stayed quiet.

'You're not the smartest man I have ever met —' he shot a cold grin in Dave's direction '— and you certainly weren't top of my list as a husband for my daughter.'

Yea, you've made that crystal clear, thought Dave. 'I don't think that's a very fair thing to say,' he choked out.

'Fair?' Michael's face was illuminated with utter disgust. 'David, were it not for the fact of my long-standing friendship with the production supervisor, you would never have had a job in the first place. Your name's dirt in this town after what happened with your brother. It was a simple job, a job for a monkey — all you had to do was keep it.'

'But the company is going under, they're laying *everyone* off,' Dave protested.

'Not everyone is being laid off,' he flared back, 'only the people not worth keeping. I have it on good authority that you were one of those people.'

It was a bitter humiliation that had reduced Dave to a speck. *He* knew how hard he worked. But there was nothing he could say. He loved June too much to argue with her father — and it was still that same love for her that made the sting of those cold words, *Stand up for what?* drive him to the pub.

Almost five hours later, just after two in the morning, June was woken up suddenly.

There was an awful commotion coming from outside the caravan. Men's voices could be heard shouting, and none of what they were saying was pleasant. Immediately June grabbed Mattie up. He was only a one-year-old baby, sleeping, but he charged her with strength.

With Mattie in one arm, June lunged from the caravan. Outside were three men, standing over Dave.

'Leave him alone,' June screamed at them.

But the men ignored her as they kicked at Dave's body where he lay in a heap against the rear caravan tyre.

Dave wasn't moving. He'd cocooned himself into a protective ball, but the three men were still giving him a beating.

June felt helpless, calling out as tears rolled down her face, Mattie crying in her arms.

Dave's blurred eyes were scanning in every direction. It seemed sure he was going to die: if the three men were willing to keep beating him in front of his crying wife and child then they were willing to beat him to death. A faint yellow light was coming from somewhere behind June, like a beacon in the night.

Suddenly a rifle sounded. One round, then silence fell. The three men turned. They were familiar with the sound.

'Lay another hand on that man and, as God is my judge, I'll put a bullet through each of your thick skulls.' Michael stood above them all, barefoot, in pyjamas, and brandishing an old hunting rifle.

Dave squirmed in agony on the ground. The three men were still poised over him, still fired up and ready to start again. Clearly they didn't scare easily: Michael was holding them at gunpoint, but they could probably overpower him.

'Mister, you should teach your son a bit of manners,' one of them snarled.

'He's no son of mine,' Michael retorted. June looked

at her father in distress. Mattie was still crying, much louder than before.

It was a stand-off. They all seemed frozen, watching.

Finally, the same man spoke again.

'All right. We've no fight with you, old man.'

Turning slowly, he looked down at Dave, who was still huddled on the ground. With utter disgust the man spat on him. Then he signalled the others, and they all disappeared into the darkness.

June rushed to Dave. 'What did you *do?*' She kissed his face and tried to soothe his wounds. 'What did you do?'

'Yes, David, what did you do this time?' Michael's words were bitter and they even seemed to catch at Mattie, who stopped crying to listen.

'He can hardly talk, Dad, leave him be.' June felt the flush rising in her cheeks.

Dave kept his head held low as June grappled him to his feet.

'They beat you so bad, Dave, so bad,' June whimpered, looking at Dave's bleeding head and bruised body. But he remained silent. 'And your eyes, oh my God, they're both already black!' June touched Dave's face and he winced. His nose was obviously broken.

'Awh.' Dave's eyes welled up with pain. 'Be careful —' But then, seeing the regret in June's eyes, he groaned, 'Sorry, love.'

'Take Mattie.' June suddenly placed the baby in Dave's arms. 'You'll feel better.'

'I don't know if I can hold him ...' Dave's bruised and aching body seemed to sag.

But June had an instinct for the best course of action — no matter how bizarre. Mattie stared at Dave curiously, his big blue eyes meeting his father's with a positive glimmer of wonderment. Suddenly Mattie broke into childish gurgling and threw Dave a smile as he wriggled, lively in his arms. And then Dave broke down in tears of pain and sorrow but, even more, of happiness, happiness at being alive.

'Tell us what you did, Dave,' insisted Michael again. 'I can smell the whiskey stink off of you from over here.'

'Daddy,' shouted June, 'this isn't the time, we'll talk about it in the morning.'

'No. We'll talk about it now, or believe me when I say it, your disgrace of a husband won't pass through my front door again for as long as I live.'

'*Daddy*.' June was appalled.

'Don't you Daddy me.' He stayed focussed on Dave. 'What have you got to say for yourself, David?'

But Dave was like a defenceless animal, cornered and alone, ears ringing. At first he stared at Michael, as if he could work the man out, or find a response to defend himself with. Then something caught his eye, something above Michael's head.

At first Dave grinned, then he started to laugh, slowly at first, gradually getting louder and more exaggerated.

'What the hell are you laughing at?' growled Michael.

'What is it?' hissed June. Dave was adding salt to an already hopeless wound.

Dave stopped laughing and coughed up a small amount of blood before he spoke. 'I'll tell you what I'm laughing at. I'll tell you what happened tonight.'

'Don't,' instructed June. 'This can wait until tomorrow.'

'No,' said Dave, 'your father has asked me what I did, so I'll tell him.'

Dave glanced up at the house, just above Michael's head, before speaking again. 'I did have a few drinks tonight, actually I had probably one too many drinks.' He laughed again, which inflamed Michael.

'You're nothing but a drunk and an imbecile.'

Dave continued, though, coughing occasionally as he spoke. 'It got quite late and I was very drunk so I decided it was time to go.' He paused to take a giddy breath; he was very pale. 'I wasn't long out of the bar when I met those men who beat the shit out of me. Do you know who they were?'

June knew exactly who the men were; everybody knew those men.

'I'll tell you who they were.' His speech was slurring with the drink. 'They were the loving fathers of the little fucking Smullins gang boys — you know the kids, the thirteen-year-olds who have the town terrorised.' Dave lurched sharply at a stab of pain. Mattie almost slipped but Dave kept his hold.

'I'm all right,' he insisted as June reached out.

Dave took another deep breath. 'The Smullins boys, the worst fucking excuses for human beings in this cesspool of a town.'

'Dave, let's talk tomorrow,' urged June.

He calmed himself. 'Anyway, I was walking down the alleyway towards home when I came across the three men. They were all drunk and were with their sons. There was a young girl lying on the ground and the men were cheering as their boys took turns doing things to the woman.' Dave flushed and looked uneasy. 'I know who she is, her name is Mary Brennan. The poor girl must have been on her way home after babysitting.' Dave couldn't contain his sorrow. 'She was just lying there, almost naked and they'd done things to her, terrible things.'

'Mary Brennan, oh my God, oh goodness …' June was horrified.

Michael showed no sympathy.

'I shouted for the police, I screamed my lungs off and that's when the guys came for me.'

June was in utter shock; her mind was racing at a million miles an hour.

'They could have killed you. I can't believe it. Come on in, no more talking —' June pulled at him gently. 'You poor thing, come in. For God's sake Daddy, you need to call the police.' She wanted to tend to Dave's wounds, to get him to lie down, to rescue him from her father.

'You are a liar, David,' Michael suddenly exclaimed. 'I don't believe a word from your thick, stupid mouth.' Michael stepped down and came towards Dave, until they were an arm's length away from one another.

'A spineless coward like you wouldn't come to the aid of a woman.'

'Daddy! He's not a coward and you've no right talking to him like that. Why do you always have to do this, why?'

Dave looked gently down at Mattie, then back to June and her father. 'Michael, do you know what the funny thing is, though? All the time when those men were beating the life out of me, I kept seeing a yellow light. They beat me for about ten minutes before June here woke up. Do you know what that light was?'

Michael turned on his heel and started to head back into the house.

'Do you know what it was, Michael?' Dave raised his voice, then pointed to the window in the house above. 'It was the light from your bedroom, where you stood and watched until you heard June's voice.'

June gasped in shock.

'It's true and your father knows it.'

Michael looked back at them; his steely expression remained. Angrily, June had dropped a heavy hand upon Dave's aching shoulders, and at last he climbed into the caravan.

As the caravan door shut, June saw her father's back, and the dim yellow light of his bedroom above.

Dave was putting Mattie back in his cot.

'You're in such a bad way,' said June. 'Maybe we should get you to a hospital.'

'No, I think it's worse than it looks,' groaned Dave. 'Do you think Michael will call the police? For Mary, I mean.'

June looked out the window at the house. She saw a light on, and her mother's shadow. 'If he doesn't,

Mam will. Darling,' she said hesitantly. 'I know it's not your fault you were attacked, but maybe your drinking —'

'What?' Dave looked at her. 'Your starting this now?'

June lifted Mattie out of his cot and began to rock him in her arms.

'I'm not starting anything, Dave. You started this whole catastrophe by moaning about my dad and the van and woe is you. And in the middle of that you went off to get sloshed — and God only knows what you spent to do it. How come you never know when to stop drinking? You can never only have one or two, it has to be just enough to have you legless and making a fool of yourself.'

'Maybe if you supported me a bit more I wouldn't have to drown my sorrows.'

'Dave, you drank like this long before I ever came on the scene; don't blame me now because you have a problem with it.'

Turning away from Dave, June left the small living area of the caravan. She entered the bedroom at the back, and seconds later the door was shut and June was in bed with Mattie.

'So that's it,' yelled Dave, 'you'd rather be like your father than for once be on my side!'

'If only you weren't drunk, Dave, if only you weren't drunk.'

For the rest of that night June had felt terrible: her husband was injured in the next room but she couldn't bear to be near him. When he needed her most, she couldn't help him.

The following morning hadn't become any easier. Dave's purpling bruises were reminders of the night before, and of the argument he'd had with June.

'I'm sorry, love,' he said when he came in and snuggled down beside her. He kissed the back of her neck.

June said nothing. Mattie was still asleep beside her.

'You know I didn't mean for all of this to happen,' he explained softly. 'I just wish we didn't live here.'

June turned towards him — and immediately saw his face. Tears fell from her eyes.

'It's not as bad as it looks,' he said again.

'It is,' she interrupted and then ran a gentle hand across his injured face. 'They hurt you really badly,' she whispered. 'But you know what? You're still here, you're still alive, thank God.'

Dave's eyes lit up. 'That's what I thought last night, when you gave Mattie to me. You don't know how good it is to hear you say that,' he replied. 'I thought you'd never speak to me again.'

June shook her head. 'Dave, I love you more than anything in this world. What do you want us to do? What will make you happy?'

'Happy?'

'Yea. It's clear you're not a happy man. You're drinking more than you used to, and all the pain and disappointment comes out when you do. You're bottling up an awful lot, Dave, and I want to help you. How can we make things better?'

Dave looked humbled. But this was the time for compromise. 'Let's move out of this caravan. We can move into that council house in Moore Heights that social services have offered.'

June sat up in the bed. 'Are you sure? I know we don't exactly have it great right now but didn't you say the estate is the last place on earth you would live?'

'Aye. I think it's about time we got on with our own lives and stopped living off your father's charity.'

June wasn't convinced. 'Well, it's the second last, as it turns out. And that Smullins gang last night, and their dads, they live in that estate, don't they?'

Dave scowled. 'I know … To be honest, though, I'd rather live in an estate with them than next door to your father.'

June had to bite her lip to contain her frustration. 'All right, we'll move out as soon as the paperwork is done.'

Now a huge wave lashed at the ferry. Screams from a group of young children startled most of the other passengers. June turned to Mattie with a grin. 'This doesn't frighten you, does it?'

'No,' he replied confidently. 'But are we nearly there?'

They were, and twenty minutes later the ferry docked in Dublin.

'Come on, grab your stuff, we've got to get off.' June led Mattie from the rocking boat to the comfort of solid ground. As she neared the exit, her heart thumped: Please, not Dad, please, not Dad!

Outside the terminal Susan was waiting to meet them. June could hardly contain her relief as they greeted each other with a huge embrace.

'Thank God you didn't bring Dad.'

'Are you joking me?' Susan smiled. 'I can hardly speak to the grumpy old codger about the weather, never mind the things that are going on for you.'

Susan stepped back from June and Mattie. 'Let me have a look at you both. My God, it's so good to have you home.'

A picture came into June's mind of Dave in England. He'd probably be just arriving home from the police station, and realising that she and Mattie were gone. She had to bite hard on the sobs to keep them in.

'Where are you parked?' she said, distracting herself.

'Not far from here.' Susan pointed the way. 'Let's go!'

1982

After the events at the caravan, Dave and June moved out as fast as they could. But documents needed processing, grants required signatures and countersignatures, and processing times were slow. Dave never spoke to Michael during that waiting period, and they avoided each other at all costs.

When at last it came time to move, Dave's only words had been, 'I don't want anything belonging to that man in my house, nothing.' He utterly detested Michael, not only for his actions on the night of the beating but also for the rift he had created between him and June. Moving into the council house wasn't ideal but at least it gave them a fresh start.

But Dave had sighed when he and June arrived at their new neighbourhood. 'We've reached a new low.'

'Don't say that,' June replied optimistically. 'We'll make the best of it, it'll be fine.'

'You're right,' he said apologetically. 'This is only the first step.'

Dave's eyes scanned the row of houses. There were ten or fifteen of them, joined like a great factory wall. They knew the internal walls would be thin, and that their lives would be on display in their grey concrete box. He shuddered, but thought about June's courage. She'd moved here for him. Least he could do was get on with it.

It wasn't long before June and Dave were fully moved in. But when Dave arrived home from the unemployment office and found the delivery of second-hand four-poster-bed parts on the living room floor, he bristled immediately. 'Where did this bed come from?'

'Look before you get on your high horse! It's not from Dad: he wouldn't give you the skin off his back.'

Dave calmed. 'So where did it come from, who's it for?'

'It's a bed for the second room. Mattie can have it when he's old enough to sleep in it.'

Dave looked over at Mattie, who was asleep on the couch with a bottle still in his mouth. 'Has he been good for you this morning?'

'Yea, a little angel.'

Dave shook his head with both amusement and annoyance. 'Pity he wasn't like that last night. He must have woken us up about ten times.'

'I know. He's teething, poor one.' June stepped away from the pile of bed parts and approached Dave with a kiss. 'And its not like we usually have much crying to contend with.'

'You're so cute when you're dressed like this,' whispered Dave, embracing her.

She was barefoot, wearing denim dungarees on top of a white T-shirt. She always wore this outfit when she was doing any major housework and it never failed to turn Dave on.

As they kissed, Dave ran his hands down the inside of the dungarees, sliding down beyond the end of the T-shirt, across her soft warm skin and under the elastic of her knickers.

'Feeling a bit frisky, eh?' She pressed her body against his. As he moved his hand lower, June threw her head back with pleasure, and Dave kissed her neck. She let out a quiet moan — and then suddenly stood still.

'What's wrong?' quizzed Dave, still kissing her.

'I think we've got a peeping Tom.'

Mattie was no longer lying down and the bottle was discarded some place out of sight. His gorgeous blue eyes were firmly fixed on his parents, who had only been moments away from deciding where they would go to make love.

'Shit!' laughed Dave, removing his hand from inside June's pants and then directing his attention to Mattie. 'Hello, little man,' he said in a bright voice. 'Do you want to help Daddy make a bed?'

The discussion about where the bed had come from never resurfaced, but June always believed that Dave knew it had come from her father's house. Maybe he's moved on from all of that rubbish, she thought.

At first June had asked her mother, 'So are you and Daddy going to get back together?' It had been almost too hard to believe that a woman so strong and so proud as her mother, at sixty-two, would decide to separate from her husband. And then it was difficult for Susan and June to listen, sitting in June's poky council-house kitchen before their mother left for Mayo, as she tried to explain why she was going.

'Why did you think I gave you that bed?' quizzed her mother. 'I no longer had a use for it.'

June looked baffled.

'Your father and I have never really seen eye to eye and, if the truth be known, we've scarcely had a single thing in common.' She paused to look at her daughters. 'Except, of course, you two!'

Anne continued to talk and, as June watched her, she saw a different woman from the one she'd called Mother all her life. In one sense it was wonderful to see her liberated from a lifetime of shackles; but the ease with which she spoke now was so unlike the quiet reserved person she'd been that there was something disturbing about the conversation — until June realised: this was not a mother–daughter chat, it was a frank discussion between women. June couldn't remember any other time when they'd spoken like that.

'Your father has forever held me back and made me feel like I was always second-best, and that's not what marriage is all about.'

'Why have you never told us this before?' asked June. 'Has something happened to push you over the edge?'

'No, there's nothing.'

'Dad will be useless without you.' June felt foolish saying this and a sharp look from Susan only heightened the ridiculousness of it. Despite everything that had happened, though, particularly between Dave and Michael, she still had feelings for her father and she feared he would crumble without Anne. But her parents were separating and there was no more to it.

'You girls need to keep charge of yourselves, don't end up like your poor old mother, realising you've let your life pass you by.' Anne looked at June and spoke quite rapidly: 'June, David is a lovely man, contrary to what your father feels, but for God's sake, watch him and his drinking. I know he'd sell the world for you and Mattie but when he's drinking he's nothing but a fool and the worse fool you'd be to accept that kind of life.' Before June had a chance to respond, Anne looked to Susan. 'You, my girl, need to find yourself a man and settle down. The way you've been parading yourself about town is disgusting. It's no wonder you have bad things said of you.' She paused for a second to choose the right words: 'I hate to say it, Susan, but your father is right — it's about time you started acting like a responsible adult.'

Silence followed. Neither daughter was fearless enough to speak out. Susan was seething, June could tell, and tight-lipped. So finally June had asked her question again: 'Are you and Daddy going to get back together?' And then she'd felt even more foolish.

'No, June.' Anne was quiet and unemotional. 'We no longer have a life together and I am very happy with that. I'm going to move in with your Aunt Geraldine and start living on my own terms.'

That last statement ran through June's head for days afterwards. What was her mother going to do differently, on a day-to-day basis as a single woman, from what she already did with Michael? As a married couple they had long been sleeping in separate bedrooms. 'He snores too much, your father,' was the original excuse, but when the snoring miraculously disappeared, the new sleeping conditions didn't revert. So Michael worked all day, arrived home for dinner and was in bed by eight: they hardly saw each other. She obviously can't stand to be around the man any more, June thought.

It was a scary prospect for her and Dave, that a lifetime of ups and downs could one day find them, in their sixties, living separate lives, wondering why they didn't realise sooner that they were unhappy. She thought about Dave, and their fresh start, and what he'd said a few nights earlier.

'This is worse than living in your parents' caravan,' he'd grumbled one evening when the estate had got under his skin. 'Listen to those idiots next door fighting again, every night it's the same bloody thing, would they ever catch themselves on and give it a rest.' He thumped violently on the thin wall in frustration.

'Don't do that,' fretted June. 'Jack next door has a terrible temper. He'll be in here fighting with you in a minute if you're not careful.'

Dave sighed; he knew she was right. 'I'm just so sick of it.'

June went back to sewing the hems of Dave's trousers.

'Does this not bother you?' There was hostility in his voice. 'Dogs, arguments, sex — it's not an *estate*, it's a camp! But you never seem to care when I talk about it.'

June looked up. 'Dave, why do we have to talk about this again. You know full well that it bothers me, it bothers me a lot. But it's not healthy going on about it all the time. What's the point, what's the alternative?'

'The alternative? The alternative?' Defeat crossed his face. 'There is no alternative, that's the problem. This place is a slum and the council has moved every scumbag in town in here. Have you looked beyond our cement backyard lately? What have we got out there? Nothing! All I can see is filthy streets and the backyards of the people across the road. You and I are better than this estate.'

'And that's why this is only temporary,' interrupted June, firmly positive. 'You'll get a job and we'll move on ... You know, I hear all of them down at the dole queue, chatting away like a pack of old women about how the country has done them wrong and about how the situation's getting worse by the day — it just sounds to me like every one of them is loving the fact that they've got something in common, a little drama to moan about.'

Dave shrugged his shoulders. 'That's nonsense.'

'Even when somebody *gets* a job,' she continued, putting away her needle and thread, 'they're not happy, they moan that the money isn't worth taking, that the job is beneath them. It's like they can't bear to leave their little club house.'

Dave was disappointed. 'That's a typical comment from somebody who came from money!'

June rolled her eyes and tossed Dave's trousers in his lap.

June and Dave moved Mattie from his cot in their bedroom to the four-poster when he was just two years of age. It had been a big decision at the time.

'Do you think he's too young?' asked Dave as he prepared Mattie's new bed.

'Maybe.' June buttoned up a new pillowcase displaying spaceships and planets. 'But we're tiptoeing around our bedroom every night. It's ridiculous — if we so much as cough he wakes up.'

Baby Mattie was a light sleeper and in the two years since his birth, Dave and June had seen their private life disappear. To chat without interruption, engage in romance, or simply sit in one another's company saying nothing at all — these times were now few and far between. In the beginning, surviving on barely any sleep and sacrificing all their time was only to be expected: a baby was a huge change in anyone's life. And everybody had an opinion, everybody had advice — but the sum of all that chatter was that life would never be the same again, and you simply had to adjust, get on with things. After two years, though, when the dust had finally settled and home life was restored — Mattie was well and truly a part of them, and Dave and June hardly remembered a time when he didn't exist — the toddler was still waking up at five every morning, his tiny mouth bellowing louder than Dave or June had ever imagined and with a shrill tone that became more striking the longer he remained unseen to. Dave and June would often lie very still, hoping that if Mattie thought they couldn't hear him, perhaps he would go back to sleep. It never seemed to work though, and with the wafer-thin walls of the council houses, their baby was waking the neighbours too.

'Are you having problems with your little one?' their next-door neighbour asked June one day, in a slightly condescending voice.

'No,' replied June warily.

'Are you sure? Maybe he's had colic, or is teething ... Have you tried rubbing a little bit of whiskey on his gums before he goes to sleep at night? That helped me when my children were at that age —'

'What are you implying, Shelley?' June was blunt, much more plain-spoken than she intended. She was exhausted. It had been weeks since she'd slept for anything longer than five hours and her defences were shattered. It wasn't going to take much to upset her.

Shelley regarded June with concern. 'Now, June,' she said softly, 'I know you're very tired, these are difficult times for you and Dave. If ever you want a break, all you've got to do is knock on my door and I'll take your boy for an hour so that you can have a rest.'

June stepped back, her tired eyes focussed intently on her neighbour. She hardly knew this robust lady with the freckled cheeks and the short auburn hair. They'd not shared more than five words since June and Dave had moved in. Suddenly, without her knowing they were coming, tears began to fall from June's blue eyes.

'Ah, there's no need for that ...' Shelley stepped closer and took June in a warm embrace. 'These are all just chapters, some are hard to read and others you fly through!'

June rubbed her eyes. She felt exposed and weak, but the hug was comforting and now she felt like she wasn't the only mother in the world who struggled with the job.

'We've all been there, June,' continued Shelley. 'Children push us to the limits.' She stepped away and placed her hands on June's cheeks, gazing right into her eyes. 'The main thing you've got to realise is that you don't have to be some kind of Superwoman, you can take advice and you can ask for help.'

June still had tears in her eyes. She couldn't believe she'd got so upset like that, but the day suddenly appeared bluer and the sunlight felt warmer.

'Is your mother still alive?'

'Yes,' sniffed June.

'I've never seen her around.'

June understood where Shelley was heading.

'She'd love to come around more, but she lives in Mayo. She and Dad are separated.'

'What about your father? Could he not come around here and help out a bit?'

June hesitated. 'Ah, there's a bit of history between Dave and my dad, they don't see eye to eye.'

Shelley perked up; she had no desire to further upset June. 'That's a pity, but not the end of the world. You remember, if you need a break you come knocking on my door. And in the meantime, give the whiskey a try — if he's teething it'll do the trick.'

It was later that day that June had decided it was time for Mattie to sleep in his own room.

'How do we do this, how can we make him stay in the bed?'

It was past seven in the evening and Mattie had just fallen asleep on the couch downstairs.

'We carry him up and just put him into the bed,' replied June with determination. 'Simple as that.' Her earlier conversation with Shelley had recharged her. She *would* regain control of her life. From now on, while Mattie slept, she and Dave could pretend they were still the couple they used to be. June knew this was more a fantasy than anything else, but she wanted to explore that fantasy.

Dave carefully leant over the couch, tucked one arm under the sleeping child and, with a jolt from his legs, lifted Mattie up against his chest and stood up.

'I understand why he should sleep in his own room, but he could still have his cot — he doesn't have to sleep in a bed. What happens if he falls out?' Dave spoke in a whisper, the lilt in his voice exaggerated by worry and tiredness.

'It'll do him good. He's old enough to be out of the cot.' June was always decisive — and determined. She gestured with her hand for Dave to move. 'Go, before he wakes up.'

'I'm going,' moaned Dave under his breath. He crossed the living room and climbed the creaky stairs.

Carefully Dave pulled back the bedclothes and lowered Mattie into the corner of the bed nearest the wall. June stood by the doorway observing.

'What are you looking for?' she whispered. Dave was scanning the floor, looking in all directions.

'One second,' he replied, raising a finger. 'This will do!' He reached under the bed and pulled out a soft teddy bear of Mattie's.

June smiled.

'It's not for him,' explained Dave, 'it's for the bed.' With a quick movement, Dave raised the mattress and rapidly placed the toy underneath, overhanging slightly on the outside. Mattie shuddered a little, his eyes opening briefly — but to the delight of his parents, he settled back into sleep at once. Dave and June remained perfectly still until they felt enough time had passed, and then they slipped away from the room.

'You nearly woke him up, what were you doing?' said June.

'I was lifting the mattress up at an angle: it might stop him from falling out.'

The worry on Dave's face was comforting to June. On those days when he had work and she was alone at home with Mattie, she sometimes felt so vulnerable, as though she hadn't a clue what was the right or wrong thing to do. Dave was feeling that way too and she loved him for it.

'Sorry I was fussing.' June grabbed hold of Dave's hand. 'I just had one of those days today.'

She didn't need to explain; Dave had seen the strain in his wife's face when he arrived home, and he'd even recognised that she'd been crying: her brilliant blue eyes had lost their sparkle. 'Don't worry, love, you can fuss all you want. I'd be fussing too if I was left home every day. It's hard work looking after Mattie, he's a live wire from the minute he wakes to the minute he sleeps.'

Late that night, June was woken up by a sound. It was not a threatening noise, just something loud enough to break her from her dreams. She turned to ask Dave if he'd heard it too, but he was no longer in the bed. She heard the sound again; it was snoring. June rose sleepily and followed the sound along the hallway. There, sitting in the doorway of Mattie's room with his head cricked over and his body in an uncomfortable-looking slouch, was Dave, fast asleep and snoring quietly.

April 1980

Stephen waited in the car with the radio playing softly. He'd been there for over an hour already and still there was no sign of Dave. He was fidgety, and drummed on the steering wheel intermittently; there was a lot on his mind. He'd had suspicions about Dave for a while, but hadn't been able to fit the pieces together until today.

'Where's Dave?' Stephen had asked Johnny earlier.

'Not sure. He said he was going out to ring your sister, but that was ages ago now. Maybe he's off with June.' It was a Sunday afternoon, two months after Dave and Stephen had moved down South. Nothing much was stirring in the house and perhaps it was the TV or the sheer mundanity of the afternoon that loosened Johnny's tongue.

'What?'

At first Johnny didn't realise what he'd said — but the strain in Stephen's voice alerted him. There was something wrong. He looked up and answered again, slower this time, but certain he was simply repeating his previous answer. 'I said, maybe he's off with Susan.'

'No, you didn't,' said Stephen sharply. 'You said he was off with June.' Stephen approached him, his height suddenly much more apparent.

Johnny stammered a reply: 'Did I? It must have been a slip of the tongue — I meant *Susan* of course.' He turned away from Stephen; suddenly it was difficult to maintain eye contact. Staring blankly ahead, Johnny tried to fake interest in the television but Stephen stood there and kept his eyes fixed on the back of Johnny's head. The tension was palpable, and Johnny was unable to maintain the charade.

'Stephen!' He turned around suddenly. 'What's your problem?'

Stephen clenched his fist, to contain the fire rising inside him — and this sent fear running through Johnny.

'Don't threaten me, Stephen,' he said then in a strangled voice. 'I've done nothing wrong.'

'Are you sure about that?' Stephen looked as though he could explode at any time.

'Look, Stephen, what do you want me to say? It was

a simple slip of the tongue, it doesn't mean a thing, for God's sake. You Finch boys are so paranoid.'

'Johnny, would you ever give your imagination a rest and just tell me the truth about what's been going on?'

'I don't know what's going on. I don't know what you're talking about — you need to catch a hold of yourself.'

'Catch a hold of *myself*,' exclaimed Stephen. 'It's *you* who needs to get a grip, keeping secrets like you're back in primary school. Grow up, for Christ's sake.'

Johnny rose to his feet and sheepishly headed towards the door.

'Where do you think you're off to?' Stephen followed him and pressed a heavy hand against the wooden door, preventing it from opening.

'Let me go, Stephen. I can't talk to you when you're like this. I don't know what to tell you. You need to calm down.'

Johnny knew what Stephen was capable of when he lost his temper. He'd seen him knock a man twice his size to the floor with a single punch, and that was over a simple spilt beer.

'I am calm,' hissed Stephen. 'You just tell me how long he's been going out with her behind my back, and I'll get out of your way.'

Johnny reflected for a moment and then answered, 'Honestly, Stephen ... This is between you and your brother. I don't want to get involved. Anyway, what difference does it make how long he's been seeing her or when it all started? So what if they're together, what do you care? You said it yourself — that you and her were going nowhere, that it was all over.'

'That's not the fucking point, Johnny.' Stephen slammed his hand hard against the door. 'I'm his brother, his flesh and blood. You don't do that — steal a girl — brothers don't do that.' But Stephen's words ended with an air of defeat, as though he'd already lost something that he truly wanted to keep. Johnny relaxed.

'Stephen, I still don't see what the big deal is. If you weren't seeing her, why can't he?'

'Because I loved her!'

'You hardly knew her, and she wasn't interested in being with you.'

'But that doesn't mean that I'd finished trying, trying to win her over.' Stephen looked away and ran his hands through his hair in frustration, as he worked through the thoughts circling in his head. Johnny remained at the door in silence. If he had words of consolation he would have spilled them, but he had nothing left to say. He knew what would happen next.

Abruptly, Stephen brushed by Johnny, hurrying

down the hallway and out of the house with a loud slam of the door.

'Don't do anything stupid, Stephen,' cried Johnny, but Stephen was already climbing into his car. Moments later Johnny heard tyres kicking up dirt, and the whirr of rapid traction.

Stephen sped down the uneven country road, plucking over the earth as he whizzed by. But from his window he saw nothing: his mind was engrossed in detailing recent events, in trying to remember *when* it might have happened.

'Stephen.' June's voice came to him as clear as though she was beside him in the car now. 'I don't think we're ready for that.'

It had been on their third date and it was only a goodnight kiss. But Stephen knew exactly what she meant. He dropped his hands slowly from her shoulders and stepped back, a little embarrassed. Smiling gently, he said, 'You're not keen on me, are you?'

June reached out for Stephen's hands. She had no desire to mock him or hurt his feelings. 'I think you're a beautiful man, Stephen, but I don't think I'm ready for a serious relationship yet.'

So Stephen had acted playfully, raising his eyebrows as he spoke. 'Not ready for a beautiful man, what's the world coming to?' She was taken by his charm and smiled, which prompted Stephen to go further. 'But I love you, June.' He spoke almost in a whisper. It was the first time he'd ever uttered such words to a woman and he felt exposed.

'How could you?' Her answer was immediate and she began to walk as she talked. 'You hardly know me — we've been on three dates!'

Indeed, it was as much a shock to Stephen as it was to June: he couldn't believe he'd been so quick to fall, the Lord knows it had never happened to him before.

'There's just something about you, I can't put my finger on it, something rare.'

'Would you go on out of that,' she replied with a blush.

She was beautiful, there was no questioning that — but it was her spirit, the glow that existed beneath the surface which made her so very different from anyone he'd ever encountered before. Stephen wasn't the first person to notice it either.

'You're an angel,' exclaimed Stephen as they walked. June rolled her eyes. 'Honestly, I don't know what it is about you but you just do something to me. I've been with so many women and I don't think I've ever cared about any one of them until you came along.' He spoke without romance, simply stating the facts.

June looked at him curiously. 'That's quite a compliment!'

'You know what I mean,' persisted Stephen. 'Look, I know that that didn't sound great — so many women and all — but it's the truth. At least I'm being honest with you.'

Stephen stopped walking. Realising he was no longer beside her, June turned back to face him. The evening was still, the night sky clear and filled with stars. Her parents' house was one of three in this small cul-de-sac on the better side of town.

'Don't rule me out so soon, June.'

June sighed. 'I don't think it's a good idea to string somebody along.'

Stephen, never one to quit, thought he sensed a weakness in June's armour. 'Lead me, I don't mind.' He was back to his cheeky antics, the lines and fighting attitude that had served him well in the past. 'I'll do you a deal — if I go home to my lonely, empty bed tonight,' he grinned, 'then you'll meet me at the pub tomorrow night. I'll bring my brother and a few friends from work. You'll love my brother — he's a great guy, not as handsome as me, but hey, we can't all be born lucky.'

June turned away and continued to the front gate of her home.

'Is that a yes?'

'We'll see.' She walked up the short driveway and unlocked her front door. She didn't look back before entering the house. She knew already what her decision was, and she had no desire to encourage Stephen any further.

June didn't come to the pub the following night. 'She never had any intention of being there,' he grumbled to himself later. He'd waited for hours, sitting on his drinks, hoping that she would arrive, while at the same time enduring Dave's displays of bum-pinching drunkenness. When eventually he trailed out after Dave, who'd been asked to leave by the management, he had accepted his defeat — and were it not for Dave's constant questions the next day, he would never have suggested trying to arrange the double date.

'I didn't see you down the pub last night,' he began when he phoned. 'We had a good time.'

'Yea, sorry, I couldn't come.' June's voice hung on the telephone line. The call was awkward and she really didn't have much to say. Also it wasn't very professional, as a secretary, to be receiving personal calls during work. 'I really have to go, Stephen, my boss could come back any minute.'

'I know, sorry,' he said hastily. 'Look, the reason I'm

calling is to see if you and your lovely sister would like to come out with me and my brother — purely platonic of course!'

Under pressure, but still much to his amazement, she agreed.

So they'd all met at Rhyslees, a popular bar in Stonebridge where you were certain to find a band belting out your favourite tunes every weekend. In the beginning the conversation was sparse. Stephen felt a little uncomfortable around June, and Susan and Dave were strangers. Soon though, with the drinks flowing, everybody's preconceptions and apprehensions began to fade away. The chatter livened up as the music became louder and Rhyslees began thumping with people streaming onto the dance floor.

'Who wants to dance?' Stephen was clapping his hands with excitement and wiggling as he rose to his feet.

'Yea, let's get this party started,' cried Susan enthusiastically, her shapely body swinging towards Stephen. He twirled her around and brought her to a stop with his hands on her hips.

June and Dave had been in mid-conversation. 'We'll follow you out in a second,' said Dave, 'and then I'll show you all how to dance.'

Susan was shoulder-dancing eagerly.

June laughed, watching her. 'We'll be there soon.'

Stephen and Susan disco-danced their way onto the floor.

'He's a little rascal, your brother.' June was watching Stephen's lively hands explore Susan's willing body on the dance floor. Stephen grinned back at the two of them. It didn't concern him much that his brother was sitting talking with June; he knew that Dave never enjoyed dancing.

'Ah, that's Stephen all right,' agreed Dave. 'But he means no harm, he just likes to have a good time.'

'Oh, don't worry,' she said with a smirk as she observed her sister dancing provocatively, 'Susan will give him a good run for his money.'

Dave's face was a little flushed; the alcohol was starting to have an effect, although he was conscious about containing himself in front of the ladies.

'So, you were saying that you like to sing?' June wanted to return to their talk, the easy flow that had started between them.

'Yes, I love singing. I'm no Elvis Presley, mind you, but I've been known to do a reasonable attempt at a song or two.'

'Like what?' June saw the bashfulness come over Dave; it was endearing.

'Ah, you don't want to know,' he replied modestly.

'Let me hear one.'

'You know, I had a feeling you were going to say that.'

'Go on, don't be embarrassed.'

Dave smiled. Despite being a little nervous, since he very rarely sang in public, he was sure that he was up to the task. The question was, what song? He looked at June's eyes, their bright contrast to her long brown hair and olive complexion.

'I shouldn't say this,' he remarked, 'and please don't take it in the wrong way, it's not a come-on or anything because I know you and Stephen are going steady — but do you know that you have the most brilliant eyes?' He shook his head as though brushing off a rush of dizziness and then, before June could comment, he continued, 'Anyway, how about I sing a verse of "Black Velvet Band"?'

'Stephen and I aren't going steady. We're just friends.' She was matter-of-fact.

'Oh, that's good.' Dave grinned again, coyly — and then coughed, feeling the need to break away from the topic. 'All right, the song, here we go!' Dave leant in close to June so that she could hear his voice over the sound of the band. He could smell the faint aroma of her perfume as it emanated from her slender neck.

Last night as I went awalking,
not intending on staying for long,
I met a frolicsome damsel
as she came atipping along.
Oh her eyes they shone like diamonds,
you'd swear she was queen of the land,
and her hair hung over her shoulders,
tied up with a black velvet band.

Dave repeated the last line, lilting slightly to signify the end. June turned suddenly, her face within inches of Dave's. Neither of them moved for a moment, their eyes locking with curiosity.

'It feels like I've known you all my life,' whispered Dave.

'I know, I was thinking the exact same thing.'

'By the way, your eyes look even better close up.'

June smiled. 'You Finch boys are a pair of charmers.' She looked away to the dance floor. 'And by the way, great singing!'

'Ah, don't be having me on.' Dave took a sip from his beer and laughed, but June remained serious.

'Well, it's your sister that's having you on.' She overstated the last three words, as they weren't a common expression for taunting in Southern Ireland.

'Dave, you've a very warm, soulful voice. I loved hearing you sing.'

From the dance floor, Stephen was beckoning. 'Come on!' he called, and he tried some fancy footwork, hoping that June would be impressed.

'I suppose we better get out and show them a thing or two, before Stephen starts doing the splits.' Dave reached for June's hand and, after a quick gulp from his beer, walked her out onto the floor.

At the end of the evening the two brothers walked June and Susan home and Stephen couldn't resist the urge to speak privately with June one last time.

'So would you like to go to the pictures with me tomorrow?' he'd asked.

'No, thank you, Stephen,' she paused. 'I have plans. I'm sorry but I'm just not interested. You and I aren't right for each other.'

Her words were final, and he had repeated them the following morning to Johnny over breakfast.

'Ah, it's for the best, Stephen, there's plenty more fish in the ocean,' Johnny had consoled.

'Yea, you're probably right — and anyway, her sister Susan isn't half bad either.' But he couldn't forget June.

Time continued to drag now as Stephen sat waiting in his car. For over two hours he'd been drumming on the steering wheel, switching from one radio station to the next and generally becoming more and more impatient. June's family home was in clear view, but in the time that Stephen had waited, there had been no activity.

'Come on,' he moaned. 'You've got to walk her home sooner or later.'

He wasn't quite sure what he was going to do — he hadn't thought things through. One thing was for certain though, he was going to confront Dave.

Finally, two people appeared in his rear-view mirror. He looked carefully. Yes, it was Dave and June.

Straightaway Stephen was uptight. He could hardly bear to see them together. He shook his head violently, livening himself up after the long wait — and opened the car door.

He stood on the footpath, facing them as they walked easily, unsuspectingly, home. At first, Dave and June were too absorbed in each other to notice him waiting, up ahead, with his rage.

'Even if Francie is right and Stephen and I do have to leave for England tonight, I'll come back and get you,' Dave was saying to June.

'I just can't believe that Stephen could get mixed up in all of that.'

'Believe me,' replied Dave abstractedly, 'neither

could I. But one good thing has come out of it all — it brought us together.'

'David, David Finch!' At Stephen's roar the two lovers looked ahead.

'Is that Stephen?' June already sounded worried.

'Ah shit, it is.'

And like a tyrant bull, Stephen hurtled towards them.

'Stephen, wait!' cried Dave fearfully as his brother bore down on them. 'Stop, now. Listen! You're in danger, Stephen. We have to leave — they're coming to get you —'

But Stephen wasn't listening: nothing was going to stand in his way.

'Oh my God, Stephen, no!' June cried out in desperation, and Dave thrust her fast to the side.

All it took was one almighty blow. Dave was rendered powerless — crashed to the pavement like a dead weight.

June regained her footing awkwardly, and in the face of Stephen's fury. He was still charged and ready to fight. 'Stand up, you back-stabbing bastard,' he yelled at Dave. 'Get up and face me like a man!' But there was no response — his brother's body was still and lifeless.

'What have you done?' screamed June, brushing past him, blind to his rage now.

The back of Dave's head had hit the ground first, smashing into the pavement. June scrambled down onto her hands and knees. 'He's not waking up!' she shouted to Stephen. 'He's not *waking up*.' She began to cry, rising to her feet and charging at Stephen, thumping his chest and slapping him powerfully across the face. 'How could you do this? How could you do this to your own brother!' Stephen stood like a statue, oblivious, dazed by what he'd done.

'Help!' June began to scream at the top of her lungs, running into the middle of the road, her eyes searching wildly in the quiet evening. From a house at the end of the street, her next-door neighbour Mrs Mac emerged, startled. Seeing June, and Dave lying there, she yelled back, 'I'll call an ambulance!' and disappeared inside.

June fell to her knees again alongside Dave. A line of blood had appeared from beneath his head and as it crept outward she became hysterical. 'Oh God, please don't take him from me, please don't take him from me ...'

Stephen's eyes welled up, he could hardly speak, he could hardly move. 'What have I done?' he finally mumbled desperately, his voice trembling. 'Oh Jesus Christ, what have I done?' Then he was struck by fear. He couldn't stay, he had to leave. 'I'm sorry, June.' His hands were shaking and his face was sickly pale. 'I'm sorry, Dave, it was an accident.' He turned and ran towards his car.

'Where are you going?' cried June. 'Come back, help your brother, you need to come back!'

The car exhaust heaved a gust of black smoke.

'*Come back.*'

But Stephen had already turned the car and was roaring past, staring straight ahead, not looking at June or Dave. His brakes screeched as he rounded the corner at the end of the street and moments later the speeding car faded to silence.

'Come back!' June's final scream disappeared into the night. There was just the distant distress of an ambulance siren.

June 1989

'So how was your ferry trip?'

Perched right up to the steering wheel, Susan was battling to see through the rain. The weather was as bad for driving as it had been for sailing, and the windscreen wipers struggled with the torrent.

June watched her. 'Since when did you start driving like an old woman? Do you think that you could you get any closer to the windscreen?'

'You try driving in this weather, and this is meant to be the start of summer,' replied Susan. 'What a joke, you can't see ten metres up ahead.' But she kept on smiling.

'You don't have to do that.'

'What?' Susan had no idea.

'You don't have to put on a bright and cheery face for me. We both knew that this day was coming.'

Susan relaxed. 'Thank God for that. Driving from Dublin to Stonebridge is going to be difficult enough without faking a smile the whole way.'

From the back seat of the Opel Cadet, Mattie was gazing off into the mist of rain belting down on the countryside. He imagined he was in a carwash machine, just like the one he and Dave went to on a Saturday morning. They always chose to stay inside the car through the wash: it never ceased to entertain them. One by one the huge electrical scrubber wheels would take turns to advance on the car, pounding like a choir of drums on the duco.

'It's like being on a merry-go-round,' Dave would yell over the noise and they'd sit together and wonder if this was the day that the scrubbers came too close to your window, and crashed through and ate you up. It was a thrill ride!

Mattie wasn't sure about how he felt to be back home in Ireland. Staring out at the rain through the fogged-up window, he couldn't stop thinking about his father, and how long it would be until he'd see him again.

'So how bad did it get?' quizzed Susan, turning to look at June.

'Keep your eyes on the road, Sue!'

'Sorry, it's a habit.' She glanced at June again then quickly back to the road. 'Sorry.'

'It got so bad that I couldn't stand to look at him any more. As soon as I saw he'd been drinking I instantly hated his guts.'

'Are you serious?'

June felt Mattie listening, and began to speak softly. 'You remember how he was here in Ireland, always the best guy in the world from Monday to Thursday, but as soon as the weekend arrived he'd go berserk with drink?'

'Yea, but he didn't —' Susan hesitated '— he didn't start beating you, did he?'

'No!' June slammed the question, but then softened her tone again. 'No, of course not, Dave's not that sort of man. I think the only time he ever hurt anyone was some loan shark who attacked his dad. Other than that, he wouldn't hurt a fly.'

Susan didn't comment. She rubbed her eyes and tried to stay focussed on the road.

'That's always been the problem, that's why I've stuck by him for so long.' June was troubled. 'He's an amazing man, but he has never known when enough is enough and he's using drink to help him deal with the past.'

'Are you talking about what happened between him and Stephen?'

'Yea.' June pondered. 'That's what's so awful about everything. I know that Dave is still hurting. But drinking isn't the answer, especially when he seems to be almost allergic to the stuff.'

Susan squinted, pressing on the brakes suddenly to allow a car into her lane, before accelerating again. 'My God, this weather is shit, you can't even see the lines on the road.'

But June was lost in her story. 'It's his mind that's the problem. When he's distracted he's fine, that's why he doesn't drink during the week.' June thought for a moment. 'But along comes the weekend and — I think he gets frightened, like he's gonna have too much time to think.'

Mattie could hear everything his mam was saying and he knew what she meant: he'd seen the best and the worst of his father also. When he was younger it had never mattered too much — it always felt like some kind of game and, what was more, he remembered his mother always joining in with the fun. There'd been lots of parties in the council house, and Mammy had got ready with a smile, and spent the nights dancing and drinking and singing with her and Daddy's friends. Now when there was a party or a night out with friends, his mam didn't have fun — she sat and looked at Daddy, and even told him off if he started being sloppy and silly. Sometimes she took a drink away from him, or grabbed Mattie and stormed off home.

But when Mattie was little, it had all been fun. Except — his heart beat a bit faster when he remembered — when Daddy started staying up all night. It became increasingly common for them to wake up on a Saturday morning, after a Friday evening out, and discover Dave still wide awake in the living room with a glass of whiskey in his hand. They'd hear him talking to himself as they entered the room but he would immediately stop to greet them.

'Dave, you're still awake,' Mammy would say.

'Good morning, my gorgeous love,' he would slur, with a huge, charming grin on his face. 'What do you want for your breakfast?' He would then rise to his feet and, with a hop in his step, make for the kitchen, to boil eggs and over-butter burnt toast.

Mattie had been three then, and he found it all vastly entertaining, especially since his father had the playfulness of a child when he wasn't sober. While Dave exuded spontaneity and recklessness, June would sit in her dressing gown at the end of their unsteady kitchen table and watch, smiling, her husband taking Mattie on a breakfast quest.

'We're boiling the eggs, we're boiling the eggs!' Daddy would sing and dance, bouncing up and down with Mattie on his shoulders, one hand supporting his son, the other cradling the glass of whiskey. Mattie knew she was petrified that in one of his twirls or aeroplane nosedives, Dave would accidentally lose his grip and send him crashing to the floor. But it never happened: though drunk, Dave kept an almost uncomfortably firm grip on his son's leg, and afterwards there'd be red marks above his foot, where Daddy's hold had been so tight it pinched.

'Butter, lots of butter, we need lots of butter on our toast!' Dave would sing to the tune of 'Day-O', and let Mattie apply the hard butter with a spoon, in huge chunks, over the bread. Then they'd all sit at the table, but Dave wouldn't eat a thing — he always lost his appetite when he drank.

'Daddy, you not do the work today?' Mattie would call out optimistically in between mouthfuls of eggs and hard toast.

'No, there's no work today for Daddy, it's Saturday,' Dave would reply and then lurch across the table and tickle the little boy. Mattie always asked the same question when he saw his father in this state, because it meant they might spend an entire day of play-acting.

One Morning when Mattie had just turned four, the usual scene was playing out and Dave was standing over by the radio, having just turned it up to listen to a song.

'This song is *the* best,' he exclaimed in an excited manner, and then started dancing, calling Mattie to join him.

The night before, June had decided to stay at home while Dave went out with a couple of the council workers he'd just been employed with again.

'Why don't we have a night in tonight?' she had pleaded with him. It had been years since he'd worked with Johnny and the boys and the time in between had seen him move like a hobo from job to job, factory work to labouring, and most recently to be the janitor at the local secondary school. Now she was afraid his old mates would notice how Dave had changed.

'It's just for a few drinks,' he replied, already getting spruced up, changing his shirt and splashing aftershave on his face.

'But you've just started working with the council again,' she appealed. 'Do you not think it's better sometimes to keep your distance a bit?' June was trying to remain calm and sympathetic. 'They say it's bad to socialise with your workmates.'

'Where did you hear that, on one of those morning talk shows?'

It was the first time June had ever questioned Dave's plans, and she was surprised by his irritation.

'Dave, don't be like that,' she chided. 'I just thought it would be good, for a change, if this one weekend we could maybe give the drinking a miss.'

Dave's eyes opened wide, almost horrified. 'What are you talking about? By the sounds of you, you'd swear we were drinking every night of the week. It's just a few beers to get the weekend started — I think we owe ourselves that much at least!'

He wasn't usually a defensive man. Usually he'd choose to retreat rather than attack when confronted. So June was puzzled.

'Dave,' she exclaimed, 'I'm just asking for one simple thing of you: that you stay home tonight. You don't have to bite the head off of me!'

'I didn't bite your head off. I don't know why you're suddenly fussing. I'm heading out. You stay at home, if that's what you want so much.'

Dave brushed by her and dashed down the stairs. They both passed Mattie in the hallway, where he sat by their bedroom door in Scooby Doo pyjamas, playing with his Lego car.

'That isn't what I want,' yelled June as she chased after him. 'What I want is for *you* to stay home for a change.'

Dave was distracted, barely hearing what she was saying as he scoured the living room for his car keys.

He turned suddenly. 'June, would you please —' He took a breath and softened his voice. 'Please relax, I really don't know what's come over you tonight.' He spotted his keys on the kitchen windowsill and grabbed them. 'Listen, love.' He faced her once again, smiling. 'Have a rest, I know you're probably tired from looking after Mattie all day. I won't be long, honestly.'

Now June was furious, but she couldn't bring herself to reply. Oblivious, Dave leant forward, kissing her warmly on the lips. 'Take it easy, gorgeous.'

And the front door shut.

'What just happened?' June asked herself, feeling shell-shocked.

That night she didn't sleep well. Neither did Mattie. 'What's with you tonight?' she whispered to him. He'd roamed the house earlier, and finally fallen asleep in bed beside her. 'You probably know that your mammy is upset ...' Taking yet another look at her watch she saw that it had reached two thirty. 'Where the hell is he?' she said through gritted teeth.

Then she lay back again and shut her eyes.

The following morning, June was in no mood to find her husband in his usual Saturday state. And that was the day of realisation for June, that Dave's behaviour was a problem.

'But Daddy has to have his big sleep, just like you did last night.'

Mattie was eager to have his playful father awake for the afternoon, entertaining him. But June's eyes had been opened. She was livid.

What time had he finally stumbled home? And since the pubs were closed after twelve, where had he stumbled home from?

Dave stopped dancing with Mattie, his bloodshot eyes were captured by the expression on June's face.

'What's wrong with you?' he asked.

'You need to sleep.' She was austere and unwavering. Maybe if he slept properly, they could start again in the evening, and rescue their weekend.

'No, he's dancing with me, Mammy,' cried Mattie, as he laughingly caught hold of Dave's wrists and swung from them. Dave held the boy's weight for a moment but then carefully lowered him to the floor. June wished that Mattie was still in bed: it was difficult having this conversation in his company.

'Why do I have to lie down?' Dave appeared strangely confused and guarded. 'I'm just dancing, I'm not hurting anyone …' He rested his glass of whiskey on the counter top, but he'd placed it too close to the edge — and it shattered across the floor, throwing tiny shards of glass in every direction. June sprang across to Mattie, who was barefoot in the centre of the kitchen, and in a single move she was holding him against her breast. 'That's why you need to lie down!' she shouted at Dave, pointing at the broken glass on the floor. 'Because it's seven in the morning and you're still stinking drunk.'

'Well, that was a bit dramatic,' sneered Dave. 'You nearly ripped Mattie's arm off over a piece of glass.'

'Dave, go to bed,' she spoke slowly, intensely, 'before you cause any more trouble.'

Dave yawned. He was actually tired, so it wasn't difficult to give in to her. 'I'm sorry, June.' He started to leave the room. 'I didn't mean to hurt anyone.'

June maintained a steely glare. 'Well, you nearly did. Now go to bed.'

Dave disappeared, and June cleaned up the mess. When she'd finished, she found her husband fast asleep on the sitting room chair. She shook her head disapprovingly. But it was better than nothing.

As Mattie drew a face in the fogged-up window of the car on their way home from the ferry, June remembered how angry she'd been that day, and how she hadn't spoken with Dave for most of the following week. And the conflict had impacted on Mattie too.

'He seems to have a lot on his mind, Mrs Finch,' his pre-school teacher had said. She had rosy cheeks and was always nice. 'Is everything okay at home?' She put the question easily, as though it was something she asked all parents she met — but June knew that this was not the case. The wide-eyed young woman who smiled a lot had an affection for Mattie, and she didn't like to see his normally good behaviour slipping.

'No, everything is fine at home.' As always June was short on matters that pertained to their private life.

'Well,' continued the teacher, trying to think of alternatives and watching Mattie playing on the floor beside them, 'perhaps it's television. These days children are extremely influenced by what they see on TV. Does he often stay up late with you and Mr Finch?'

Each afternoon, leading up to dinnertime, June would tire Mattie out by playing games and going for walks; his bath followed an early evening meal at six thirty; and there was book reading, at seven, before he'd shut his eyes and drift away. But on Friday evenings, drink and song would wake Mattie, and he'd be brought downstairs in his mother's arms to be rocked back to sleep. In the background, behind the waft of cigarette smoke and people dancing and singing and drinking, the television would be playing too, with the sound turned down. He would struggle to return to sleep and then June would rest him on the couch with a blanket and pillow.

June tensed up at the teacher's question. 'Tell me what he did wrong,' she said.

'Well, Mrs Finch, it was a truly upsetting sight, but Mattie and Niall attacked —'

'Attacked?' exclaimed June.

'Yes, Mrs Finch — attacked one of the smaller children in the class. It happened in the playground. The boy's name is Gerome. He's a quiet lad. Anyway, the two boys ran at Gerome and knocked him to the ground. I called out for them to stop but they pressed his face against the asphalt and hit him repeatedly on the back. What was worse, Mattie was the instigator.'

June was sick with shame. 'Oh my God, I can't believe he could do something like that.'

'Mrs Finch,' said Mattie's teacher, reaching across the table and touching June's hand reassuringly, 'as terrible as it all sounds, this isn't as awful as you're now imagining it to be.'

'What, so you're saying that my son doesn't have a violent streak in him?'

'That's exactly what I'm saying.' The teacher remained calm. 'I see your son every day and I've got to be honest, he's one of my favourite children. He's an honest and sweet little guy with a huge heart, and all I can say to you is this — for Mattie to do that to Gerome, something must have changed in his life.'

'What?'

The teacher sat back. 'I think he's seeing and hearing things that are upsetting him, influencing his judgement. Maybe he's not sleeping well at night — does he have nightmares? Or maybe he's watching television unbeknownst to you or Mr Finch, and it's giving him ideas. You can't watch any child twenty-four hours a day. But maybe try to see what he's doing when he thinks your back is turned?'

June and the teacher had talked a bit more that day, and June had said she'd speak to Mattie's father too.

All these years later, as Mattie sat in Aunty Susan's car on the way back home from the ferry, he remembered waking up one Saturday before his mother and, unable to go back to sleep, deciding to go downstairs to see his father, who he expected would be in the living room, awake after his night out. But when he got down the stairs, he couldn't see his father.

'Daddy,' he sang out as he skipped from room to room and past the stairs again, determined to find his father, 'can I have some eggs!'

'Daddy!' he called again. A noise came from behind him and he playfully swung around on the spot, but there was nobody there! His face dropped; he was certain he'd heard something. Mattie bit his lip. Then the noise sounded again and he stood very still. He listened carefully, ears alert. The front door was to his right now, separated from the stairs by a long window.

What is it? he wondered, and he approached the door hesitantly — and then bravely pressed his ear against it. Quickly he jumped away. He wasn't frightened though, just confused. He peered at the door handle: he was tall for his age but it was still out of reach. Mattie contemplated the problem and then remembered the stool kept under the kitchen table in case of one too many visitors. He turned and rushed off to fetch it from the kitchen, carrying it firmly in his small hands. He rested it next to the door, astute enough to see that the door wouldn't open if he was directly in front of it. Finally, after a brief, awkward climb onto the seat, Mattie stood high enough to reach across and turn the door latch.

Like almost everything in the council house, the door was flimsy. As soon as it was unlocked, it was easily swept open by the morning breeze, smacking back with a light thud. Mattie got a sudden fright and almost lost his balance — not because of the door but because of what he saw lying curled up on the welcome mat. It was his father, fast asleep.

Mattie climbed off the stool quietly. He wasn't quite sure what to do. When he was even younger, Mattie had been scolded for pouncing suddenly on June or Dave when they were sleeping, because it scared them half to death.

Mattie knew his father's slaps, while rare, were much harder than his mother's. But he knew Mammy would be furious if she found Dad asleep outside. She went mad at Mattie if he even thought about doing things in the wrong places! He made his decision. Tugging at Dave's arms, he tried to drag his father into the house. He heaved and huffed but his father was at least ten times heavier than anything Mattie could move. Then — surprisingly — Dave woke up. His tired eyes met Mattie's. He unstuck his lips, and his other hand came up to his head. Then he glanced around, first at the ground where he lay, then back at the houses and the street, and lastly, up at his house keys. They were hanging from the door, where he'd managed to insert them the night before; he must have passed out before he could turn them.

'Daddy, can you make me breakfast?' His spirits brightening, the boy gazed at his father.

Dave shook his head and sat up.

'Mattie —' He struggled to his feet, falling forward a little as he stepped into the house — 'you're up early today.' He removed the keys from the door and closed it gently. Then he took a deep breath. Though he was still quite dazed, Dave's sleep had sobered him and, for a change on a Saturday morning, he was looking alert now. He regarded his son with an appreciative smile. 'Thanks for waking me before Mammy woke up!'

'You were asleep outside,' declared Mattie.

Dave ran a hand across his stubbled face. 'I am a bit silly,' he replied, and he crouched down to whisper in Mattie's ear. 'But let's keep this a big secret. We won't let Mammy know, because she might get mad.'

'Okay, Daddy.' Mattie spoke softly, his bright face suddenly filled with concern. 'I won't tell Mammy.'

'Good boy.' Dave's face looked sad — but then he clapped his hands together. 'So what do you want for breakfast?'

When June came down that morning and entered the kitchen, she expected to see Dave in his usual state. She stood perplexed at the doorway. Dave and Mattie were eating at the kitchen table, and there was no alcohol in sight.

'When did you get home?' she asked matter-of-factly.

'Hours ago,' he replied as he poured milk into his tea. Mattie smiled up at his mother. She saw that Dave was still affected by drink, but she could also tell that he'd slept. She was puzzled, but pleased and relieved. Approaching Dave, she leant down and kissed him on the lips — much to the happiness of their little boy.

The following Saturday, Mattie woke up even earlier than the week before. Earlier than his mother again. He jumped from his bed and ran downstairs, to where his father, thankfully, was inside the house — but unfortunately wide awake with a drink in his hand, sitting on the couch.

'Good morning, Mattie! What are you doing awake, could you not sleep?' The clock on the wall said it was three forty in the morning, and the radio hummed with a daily-show repeat. Mattie just eyed his father from the living-room door, and Dave was taken aback.

'Are you okay, Mattie, did you have a bad dream?'

Mattie scratched his head, and then made a casual move towards his father. He said nothing as he approached, and Dave watched drunkenly as his son reached for the glass of whiskey he was holding, tugged it from his grasp and placed it on the wooden coffee table in the centre of the room.

'Hey, that's mine,' said Dave jovially. But Mattie put his hands on Dave's legs and urged his father to lift him into his arms, which Dave did without hesitation. Then Mattie lay back against his father's chest, forcing Dave to stretch out on the couch.

Dave smiled as he looked down on his young son, who was now resting across his body with his eyes closed. The whiskey was now too far away for Dave to reach. He'd have to wait until his son was in a deep sleep before moving him.

Dave himself fell asleep before that could happen.

At seven he woke. June was still asleep upstairs, and Mattie was nowhere in sight.

'Mattie?' he called, getting up. Not finding him in the kitchen either, Dave went upstairs, where he discovered Mattie snug and fast asleep in his own bed.

On Monday morning Mattie was still tired, yawning as he went to pre-school. But he was content. It had been argument-free on both Saturday and Sunday. So the following weekend he did the same thing again, even though he was really tired now.

As instructed by his teacher though, June was soon keeping a close eye on Mattie, and it wasn't long before she discovered his late-night missions.

'Mattie, up to bed this second!' she ordered, coming upon the boy half-asleep in his father's arms. Startled, Mattie began to cry.

'What are you doing?' cried his father in a drunken slur. 'He couldn't sleep, leave him alone.' He held Mattie close, wiping at his tears.

June approached the pair and separated them forcibly, lifting Mattie into her arms. His crying grew louder.

'Leave him, June.' But Dave was very drunk, stumbling as he rose.

'I will not,' shouted June. 'You're an absolute disgrace. Our son is getting in trouble at pre-school and it's because his drunken, good-for-nothing father is allowing him to walk the house at night. Mattie's exhausted because he doesn't sleep properly any more — and that's all your fault.'

Dave wasn't able to focus on what she was saying. He mumbled at her.

'Listen to yourself,' she continued to shout. 'You can't even string a sentence together; you disgust me. I've watched you for the last two weeks and I can't believe that you'd let your own son suffer to guilt yourself into sleeping.' June drew breath. 'Instead of pretending that you've slept all night, why don't you do us all a favour and guilt yourself into quitting, because you can't handle the drink. You're nothing but an alcoholic!'

June stormed out of the room.

Dave fell back into his chair. He was shaken — but at the same time he was too drunk to think about it, and soon he passed out.

Hours later, when he'd woken up, June's eyes met Dave's. 'You're finally awake. How's the alcoholic doing today?'

He looked at her, puzzled. He couldn't remember a thing about the night before.

The traffic on the way home from the ferry had been erratic, with other drivers making senseless manoeuvres. Susan took a hand off the steering wheel and massaged the back of her neck. At least the rain was beginning to subside.

'So did you ask him to quit drinking again?' she asked.

'There was no point. All these years, he's tried a million times and I'm convinced that each time he falls off the wagon, he gets worse than he was before.'

'I remember you telling me he quit when you arrived in England.'

'That was the deal we made — I said I'd go if he stopped drinking,' June reflected, and then was overcome with a sense of deep sorrow. 'But he can't quit, the man needs counselling. He needs Alcoholics Anonymous for his drinking and a psychologist for his troubles. Do you know how many times I've woken up to find Dave drunk and talking away to Stephen as though he was in the room?'

Susan shook her head in dismay. 'I know, I saw him myself one time.'

'Did you? When?'

'Years ago, around Christmas time. Actually it was Christmas Eve.' Her voice had brightened a little at this thought. 'We'd had a few drinks while we arranged all of Mattie's Santa gifts under the tree — remember? — it was that year I was staying with you for Christmas. Anyhow, as usual Dave was half a dozen drinks ahead of me and you. It was getting late and we decided to call it a night, but Dave wouldn't budge —'

'He never knows when enough is enough.'

'Yea. Right. He stayed up drinking while we all went off to bed.'

'Typical.'

'Anyway, in the middle of the night I woke feeling thirsty and came downstairs for a drink of water. When I came into the living room, Dave was chatting away:

'"Stephen, I love her, how many times have I got to tell you that? I've got nothing to be feeling guilty about." I can remember it exactly. "And you, you bollix, you nearly killed me with that punch!" He didn't even notice I was there. He was just looking at the empty chair alongside the Christmas tree.

'So I asked him if he was okay — but it was horrible. He didn't hear me, or see that I was there. He just said, "Look, let's just change the subject, there's nothing to be gained by talking something to death! Anyway, it's been so long since I've seen you, I don't want to argue. Tell me something, anything?" Then he stood up and pointed to the other chair and he started to laugh! "Trust you to mention something like that, I remember her well, she was good-looking —" He laughed even louder. "You're some gigolo, you had her eating out of your hands …"

'I almost panicked, I was going to wake you — but then I figured you would've probably seen it all before.'

June sighed. 'Yes, too many times.' She shivered at the thought. 'And it's so scary to watch, it's like he's in a trance or something.'

Mattie too had seen his father many times in that state, especially as he grew older. As a little child it had never seemed that strange to him: his father was just being silly. Then as a seven-year-old, these glimpses of his father became much harder to understand.

'What are you crying about, Daddy?' Mattie had come down to the living room one evening, frightened from his sleep by the sound of loud wailing.

Dave was in floods of tears, standing against the wall on the far side of the room and hitting it.

'I'm sorry,' he was crying out. 'I'm so, so sorry!'

'Daddy, what's wrong?' Mattie went nearer to his father.

'It's not my fault. I fell in love with her the same way that you did, there was nothing I could do about it. I wish we hadn't ended like we did — it's not meant to be like that, it's just not meant to be like that!' Dave was yelling by then.

Mattie reached for his father's hand, but was startled when Dave shrugged him away and continued to shout.

'Daddy,' called Mattie, 'Daddy, stop it, stop crying —'

'Stephen, you can't blame me for everything —'

'Daddy!' Mattie was getting upset, disturbed by his father's pain. Mattie's one thought by this time was to make it stop — and he knew that June was the only person who could do that. Distressed, he ran from the room.

Minutes later, he brought June in, holding her hand. But by then the room had fallen silent and Dave was lying on the couch with his eyes closed.

'He was crying, Mammy, I promise, he wouldn't stop.'

Dave was fast asleep, but leaning close to him June saw undried tears on his face.

'He's asleep now, Mattie. You were very good to come and get Mammy.'

'What was wrong with him?' asked Mattie with sorrow.

June thought about the many times she'd seen Dave in that same state, and how she'd often abandoned her anger the following morning and replaced it with concern.

'Your father has bad dreams sometimes, Mattie,' she said, 'and they really upset him.'

The Stonebridge sign had appeared on the roadside up ahead. 'Finally,' said Susan with an exhausted sigh. 'Home sweet home is just a few minutes away.'

June made no reply; she had been silent for the past ten minutes and, somewhere along the way, Mattie had fallen asleep in the back seat of the car.

'What a crazy trip,' exclaimed Susan. 'I'm telling you, June, this country is the world's worst for driving in. As soon as it rains, every dickhead decides to get into their car.' She laughed resignedly, and then June spoke.

'Home sweet home. Home sweet home! Home sweet home …'

'What's that, honey?' quizzed Susan, still watching the road.

'Home … Home sweet home, home, home. Home sweet, sweet home —'

'What?' Susan took her eyes off the road to glance at June, and immediately slammed on the brakes.

Mattie
&
Dave

June 1989

When Dave finally awoke, feeling sick on the bare mattress in a British holding cell, his hangover hit him harder than ever — she'd be gone when he got home and so would Mattie.

It was 4 pm before Dave was finally released and the hours leading to that point were unbearable. In his mind he'd visualised each and every movement she would make as she left him.

And when he finally walked from the lock-up out of town to the house, she was gone and so was Mattie. Their clothes were gone, their photographs were gone, their toothbrushes were gone.

The realisation that his wife and son had left him alone in England, was bad enough — but what made it even more painful was the fact that he wasn't permitted to leave the country to chase after them.

'I've got to go home,' he pleaded with the constable in the information booth at the police station. It was early evening and Dave had returned to the station in a state of panic.

'I was released today and by the time I got home, they'd already left for Ireland. I've got to go after them, I've got to get home!'

'I don't make the rules, Mr Finch.' The constable was burly with a thick moustache. He scanned Dave's police file.

Dave felt a knot in his stomach, a sickening feeling of regret and remorse. He knew what the constable was reading. He'd been caught driving with five times the legal limit of alcohol in his bloodstream.

'I'm sorry, Mr Finch.' The officer raised his eyes from the report. 'It looks like you've got yourself in a lot of trouble this time.' There was a queue of people building up behind Dave, and the policeman's time and patience were limited. He gestured pleasantly for the next person to come forward.

'Wait,' persisted Dave as he held back the elderly lady behind him.

She looked at Dave with contempt.

'Sorry, missus, just give me a wee second here!' Dave turned once again to the constable, who was unimpressed. 'What can I do? Help me, please. Is there anything I can do? My wife and my son are probably halfway across the Irish Sea by now — I've got to go after them!'

A family photograph was on the policeman's desk. He shrugged his shoulders. 'Look, mate,' he said in a deep London accent, 'you're in a bit of a pickle here and I would love to help you — but I can't. You have absolutely no options: you can't leave the country until your arraignment in two months' time and, I'll be honest with you, you might not be able to leave after that either. You could do time for this.'

The words hit hard, much harder than the constable had meant them to. Dave's face went sickly pale — and then without any warning, he crashed to the floor.

'What did you say to him?' a second officer cried, rushing around the counter.

The constable was already crouched over Dave. 'I said he might have to do some prison time, and the poor bugger fainted.' He patted Dave's cheeks while the other officer kept people back. When Dave came to, he saw the crowd, blurrily, and heard talking.

'Is he all right?' one voice inquired.

'He heard he has to go to gaol,' came another, from somewhere out of sight.

'You need to go home and get some rest.' This was the constable he'd been speaking with. 'I expect it'll take some time for everything to sink in. Talk to a solicitor, see what your options are …'

By now Dave could stagger to his feet with the help of the officer. 'Oh, I'm sorry about that — I don't know what came over me,' he said under his breath, feeling embarrassed and upset. 'I suppose I better go home. Thank you.'

'I think you're best doing that.' The officer saw Dave out the door, making sure he was recovered enough to go home.

But once Dave was in the street, the man appeared again.

'Mr Finch,' he called, coming down the stairs of the police station, then dropping his voice to a whisper, 'tell your solicitor to check the calibration records.' And as soon as the words were out, he disappeared back into the building.

It wasn't until later that evening, after he'd finally managed to hitch a lift home to his empty house, that the officer's words made sense. He'd been dazed earlier, but now he understood. The alcohol test mustn't have been correct.

'Why did he do that?' said Dave in wonder. 'I can't believe that somebody, *a policeman*, would do that.' He was overcome with a sense of absolute appreciation for the human spirit, that at times of desperation, somebody might come along and throw you a lifeline.

Dave rose from the kitchen table where the take-away chicken curry he'd bought had hardly been touched. The room was shrouded in darkness: three of the four fluorescent bulbs in the ceiling light had blown, and the last one flickered. Dave remembered June asking him to pick up some spares on his way home.

'It doesn't matter.' She'd smiled then, after her husband came through the door tired and empty-handed. 'You can get them tomorrow.'

But there hadn't been a tomorrow — it was the day she and Mattie left him.

Dave wandered through the two-bedroom house. It was so quiet, all its life had been snatched away by a night of lunacy. But it wasn't just one night's craziness, thought Dave, I had this coming to me for a long time. The bed in Mattie's room was still unmade and Dave could almost hear June's voice, calling again for her boy to tidy it.

Where would they be now? It might take ages before he'd hear from them, if in fact June would contact him at all. If she'd gone to the council house, there's no way Susan would let him speak to her. He had to give her some space; she needed time to clam down. What a mess I've got myself in, he thought. If only I could talk to her — I just want to hear her voice!

'I really hope that policeman has done me a favour,' he fretted aloud, then. 'I could never survive in prison.'

Back in the kitchen a bottle of Jameson whiskey stood near the stove. All evening it had caught his eye but so far he hadn't gone near it. He didn't want to drink it — but didn't want to throw it out either. Dave reached for the bottle, placing a hand on its all-too-familiar body. 'Fuck you —' he pushed the bottle roughly, sending it sliding along the bench top '— you've ruined my life.' It stopped inches from the edge.

Dave laughed sarcastically. 'Typical. I couldn't break you if I wanted to.'

In desperation he ran his hands across his face. 'What am I going to do?'

But there were still only two answers to that question: he could either flee the country before his arraignment, causing himself even more trouble — or he could wait it out and hope that June got in touch with him. He'd try writing to her, perhaps even phoning her father. If the policeman was right about the alcohol-test calibrations, Dave might get off without a conviction, and be able to go home to Ireland to win June and Mattie back.

He sat once again at the table.

'June, I'm so sorry!'

His head filled with images of her face, her beautiful skin, her eyes that could speak with a single glance. Had he stolen her from his brother? The question circled in his mind again, as it did so often. Why, after so many years, should it make any difference?

'*No*,' he declared, 'no, I didn't!' He ran his hand across the back of his head: the raised scar there was an everlasting reminder of Stephen's rage.

He thought about Johnny. How he couldn't keep his mouth shut.

But then Dave remembered June on that first night they'd spoken in Rhyslees. He thought about how awfully he'd sung, and how she'd been polite enough to give him a compliment. At the end of the night, when Stephen and Dave had walked the two sisters home, he'd whispered in June's ear, 'I'll pick you up tomorrow at one o' clock outside your house.' She'd smiled at him but gave no hint of her intentions, leaving him wondering.

'You decided to come!' He couldn't hide his enthusiasm the following afternoon as June opened the car door.

'Well, you are parked outside my house. I couldn't have the neighbours calling the police on you.' She met his warm gaze with a smile of excitement. 'So, where are you taking me?' June settled in and Dave started the car.

'You'll see.'

At first the conversation was matter-of-fact, both Dave and June wondering if what they'd felt the night before had been simply because of the drink. It wasn't until they reached Killiney Beach in Dublin that things took a turn for the better.

'I adore the ocean,' exclaimed June, stepping out of the car and walking from the car park to where the grass became sand that flowed right down to the sea.

'Yea, I found it a week after I first arrived down South ... Hardly anyone ever comes to this beach.' The sea stretched gloriously around them. 'It's like no other place on earth, it's so beautiful.'

They both stood still, looking off into the distance, watching waves crashing to the shore with an almighty rush of sound.

'Come on,' cried June, suddenly bending to take off her shoes and socks. 'Let's walk in the water.' She was wearing blue slim-fitting cords that hugged her shapely legs and worked well with her red polo-neck top. Her long hair was tied at the back, displaying the contours of her slender neck. And Dave found it hard to resist looking at her pert behind as she bent to roll her trouser-cuffs up. They reached the water together, their feet getting wet at the same time.

'It's freezing,' cried June, in quick retreat.

'You're telling me.' Dave laughed, dashing away from the water's edge with her.

As they sat side by side with their feet buried in the sand, talking, the awkwardness between them began to disappear.

'My dad's a pretty tough man,' said June openly. 'He doesn't like Susan or me dating anyone.'

'And so he shouldn't,' teased Dave. 'A beautiful young girl like yourself could easily wind up with someone terrible — worse still, a man like myself from Belfast.'

'Wouldn't that be just awful.' She smiled, but then looked away forlornly.

'But I'd say you've had enough men hanging around your door, all the same. You wouldn't be the world's worst-looking girl I've ever seen.'

June slapped Dave playfully. 'Aren't you great with the compliments.' She thought for a moment. 'I've had interest from a few men, but not nearly as many as Susan has.'

Dave grinned. 'Yea, she reminds me of my brother Stephen ... She's a bit of free spirit, isn't she?'

'That's a nice way of putting it.' June grinned. 'Ah, she's adorable, I love her to bits.'

June suddenly started squinting. The wind had picked up and sand had been blown into her eye. 'Agh,' she cried, holding her right eye open, 'that hurts!'

'Let me have a look,' replied Dave calmly, turning to face her. 'You have to stay still,' he instructed then, as she moved her head about while he tried to examine her. With a quick flick of his finger, Dave brushed the grains of sand from June's eye and then sat back. 'There you go, how does that feel?'

June smiled. 'Not bad, Mr Finch, not bad at all.'

Dave didn't seem convinced and bent towards June again, staring intently into her eyes.

'What is it?' she said, concerned, her eyes very blue in the sun.

'It's nothing, I just wanted a better look at you.' With that, Dave leant in and kissed June. She was startled initially and turned away, looking at him sharply.

'Oh — I shouldn't have done that,' he said quickly, apologetically. 'I'm sorry, I was way out of line.'

June was looking intently at him now, her expression unreadable.

'Really, I'm sorry,' he persisted, feeling more wretched the longer she stared at him.

'I'm only joking with you!' She suddenly smiled, and then leant in to kiss him back.

Ten years later, and the bottle of whiskey stood on the edge of the bench top, still trying to lure him. It had a firm hold on Dave and was distracting him from his thoughts. Again he rose, taking the amber bottle into his hands. So strong was his desire to taste the poison that Dave *had to* open it, to smell the contents. Surely that would quench his cravings!

The scent was intoxicating, as it travelled from his nose to the rest of his body. He could almost taste the liquid, the *pleasure* of it, feel it on his tongue, sense it running down his throat and instantly being mopped up by his blood vessels to course through his entire body.

Dave put the top on the bottle again and slammed it down on the counter.

'*Argh.*' He cried out at the top of his lungs again and again.

How bad have I got? He rushed to the bathroom mirror and switched on the light and faced himself. Who are you?

Then he thought, What's happened to David Finch? Where's the man who told his own father that he would never have any demons, that he would never treat his family the way his father did?

Dave bowed his head and pressed his fingers against his temples. Self-pity isn't going to help me now either — God knows I've done that before.

He remembered the countless times his drunkenness had resulted in arguments and disappointments, and how he had often scowled at himself in the mirror, declaring how disappointed he was with himself. Only rarely had it made him try quitting, and that never amounted to much.

But this time it's different, this time June has actually left me for real and I've got nothing!

Dave faced himself once again. June had left him before, but never for longer than a day. He thought of the first time. It was when Dave's weekend binge drinking had extended to Sunday night. Later June would tell him she'd always been surprised this hadn't happened before: she couldn't comprehend a compulsion that only pertained to Friday and Saturday nights. So when eventually she did find him still drunk on a Monday, she had run to one place that she had left to go — her father's.

She had never wished to involve Michael, and especially not when he was so bitter over the sudden ending of his own marriage.

'I told you he was wrong for you, did I not tell you that he would amount to nothing?'

'Dad, please don't,' she'd begged, 'I just need a night away from the madness, I don't want to have to face it here too.'

'Why didn't you go to your mother then? You knew how I would react.'

'Because Mam lives in Mayo now, which may as well be a million miles away from here, and Mattie is seven years of age.'

'What has his age got to do with anything?' Michael's venom had reached his eyes.

'He's in school now and I'm damned if I'm having him missing days because of the antics of his father. He's behind as it is.'

Susan came into the room. She was still living at home at the time, and knew how to handle her father. But June's last remark had made Michael angry.

'What do you mean, he's behind in school?'

'Hi, June,' Susan interrupted softly. 'You poor thing, come upstairs and let's talk about it.'

Susan threw a cursory glance at her father as she crossed the room and hugged her sister.

But Michael was infuriated. 'June, I want to talk about this right now.'

'Dad.' Susan gazed at him. 'Give it a rest, June doesn't want to talk to you right now.'

June was surprised by her sister; she couldn't imagine being so direct with him. But it worked. The two girls left the room, where their father remained with his livid thoughts.

Afterwards, June had told Dave all this, so he would understand that he had driven her to the last place she needed to be.

And now Dave was glaring at his reflection. His eyes were sunken, with heavy black lines beneath them, while his face was dry and grey and jaded. The Jameson was still calling to him from the other room, but he remained in front of the mirror.

He took a breath and stepped closer to the mirror. 'Do you know what we're going to do?' The intensity of his voice rose then, as the notion in his head began to excite him. He leapt back and pointed. 'We're going to go into that kitchen, we're going to grab that bottle of Jameson and fucking smash it into a million pieces on the back path!'

He had fire in his eyes.

'That's fucking *it*, I'm going to get my family back come hell or high water.'

Dave stormed into the kitchen and grabbed hold of the whiskey. Holding it at a distance like a stick of dynamite, he ran to the back door and out into the yard.

'Good fucking riddance,' he yelled as he hurled the bottle with gargantuan force against the concrete, smashing it into a million shards of glass which he kicked in all directions with his hobnailed boots. A rush of exhilaration filled his body and for a moment he was invincible and the day's events no longer existed.

When the excitement began to fade, though, the quiet house resumed its lonely state.

Dave suddenly regretted his noble gesture. Gazing down at the broken bottle, he began to run through in his mind the places in the house where there might be another one hidden — he needed a drink, he had to have a drink.

Storming inside, Dave frantically started pulling out cupboard drawers and flinging their contents across the floor. In the living room, he turned the old television set on its side to get at the wall cabinet behind; in the bedrooms the spare blankets and sheets were tossed in all directions; and in the kitchen the fridge and freezer were emptied out. Dave searched everywhere, but found nothing.

'*Argh*,' he cried again. 'Fuck!'

He fell to the ground in a defeated heap. 'This is the end,' he moaned. 'This is the end.'

January 1990

'I'm happy that Dad is back home, it feels like I haven't seen him in ages!'

It was early morning and the reunion with Dave after six months had been great for nine-year-old Mattie, and he awoke the next day ahead of everyone else, too excited to go back to sleep.

'Why don't you talk to him, Mam?' Mattie looked at his mother who sat on the kerb next to him. It was before six o'clock in the morning and the street was still enveloped in greyness.

'Aunty Susan said that Dad went away on work,' continued Mattie to his mother. 'Maybe like my friends whose dads go to Africa — they only come home every six months, sometimes just once a year.'

'I don't think he was off on work,' replied June, patting his hand.

Mattie's eyebrows rose as though he'd just heard something of great interest. 'Me neither,' he exclaimed with enthusiasm. 'When we were in England, he never said anything about going to Africa. Where do you think he was?'

'I don't know, Mattie,' she said, her voice cool and distant.

From down the street came the rattling of milk bottles, as the milkman made his morning deliveries, occasionally shouting orders to his young helper. Mattie had found their pint already on the doorstep.

'It's so early!' Mattie kicked his heels in the gutter. The night was slowly being replaced by the dark blue haze of morning. It wouldn't be long until the sun would light the sky and everyone's usual morning activities would begin again. Mattie looked up at his mother next to him — at first he couldn't see her, perhaps because his eyes had just adjusted to the light in the sky. Rubbing them with the edge of his wrist soon brought her back into view.

'Wow, I couldn't really see you there ...' But his voice wasn't overly concerned. 'I think this might be the earliest I've ever been outside.'

'There's a first time for everything!' She smiled. 'What are you thinking, Mattie?'

'Nothing!'

'It doesn't sound like nothing ...'

Mattie let out a sigh. 'It is nothing, I'm not thinking anything! Stop asking me that.'

'Don't be rude now, Mattie, you know it's not nice to speak back to somebody like that.'

'I'm not being rude.'

'Yes, you are.'

'Sorry!'

He felt her hand smooth his hair. He always loved that. 'I'll tell you what ... Can I guess what you're thinking?'

Mattie sat quietly considering this option.

'You can try, but you're not going to find out because I'm not thinking anything.'

'All right, are you *not* thinking that you'd like to see me and Daddy back sleeping together in our old bed?

'And would you *not* like to see me and Daddy being happy together and not fighting about anything anymore, especially like we did in England?'

Mattie frowned at her. 'How did you know that's what I was thinking —?' He suddenly stopped speaking, then re-phrased with a cheeky grin on his face — 'that I was *not* thinking?'

June stood up and wandered towards the next cross street. 'Mother always knows best. I'd best be off.'

Mattie grimaced: he'd only ever really heard this at

times when he was being taught a lesson, or told off for something he shouldn't have done.

On this occasion, at six o'clock on a Monday morning, mother really and truly did know best.

'So,' he continued innocently, '*are* you and Daddy going to get back together?'

But his mother didn't answer, so Mattie gave up and scrambled to his feet. 'Okay. Bye Mammy.' He watched as she turned the corner and was gone. Mattie let himself in.

'Who have you been talking to?' Dave's voice startled Mattie who leapt back against the front door.

'You scared me!' cried Mattie.

'Sorry, son,' he spoke softly. 'Have you been awake for long?'

Mattie rubbed his eyes. His early start was beginning to take hold. 'I just woke up and then I couldn't go back to sleep so I thought I'd get the milk in.' The pint bottle was cool as he handed it to his dad.

Dave nodded. 'Ah, that's no problem, I get like that sometimes. And who were you chatting with?'

'Mammy!'

Dave was startled. Images flooded to mind. Her soft white skin as she applied make-up for a night out on the town, her wide endearing smile when something amused her, the glow she got in her eyes when she was excited. It had been a long time since Dave had seen June, and there hadn't been a moment since he stepped into their old home that he hadn't thought about her. But right now, it was Mattie he needed to think about.

'Ah, your mammy, is it? Is she … is she okay?'

'She's fine, Dad.' Mattie's voice was sharp. Dave would have to tread carefuully, especially as Mattie knew exactly how he and June had left things.

'I'm surprised she's been here, Mattie. We weren't expecting her after all.'

'She was here, Daddy, I'm not lying.' Mattie was bothered. 'Have I done something wrong?'

'No, of course not, and I'm not saying that you're lying.' Dave noticed his voice had risen. He calmed himself. 'Of course you're telling the truth. I would just love to have a word with her, that's all.'

'And say you're sorry?'

Dave looked at Mattie, who looked back defiantly. Then the boy slipped past him and up the stairs, slamming his bedroom door behind him.

Dave grunted with frustration and went to the kitchen to put the milk away. Nine years old, he thought. He remembered how he'd slept outside Mattie's room for an entire week when they first moved him to his own bed, each night intent on ensuring his little boy had a peaceful, uneventful sleep. He hadn't told June what he'd been doing ... but she must have known. She was especially nice to him on each of those mornings, laying on a big breakfast before he set off to work.

He's not a little baby now. Dave put the kettle on, and his thoughts returned to June, how he wished so much to talk with her.

Susan was only half awake when she entered the kitchen.

'Morning!' Dave was sitting at the table.

'Oh — I got a bit of a fright, seeing you there,' said Susan. 'It's just been Mattie and me for so long now.'

She returned his smile and then made a side-sweep across the kitchen, tying up her dressing gown as she walked. In front of the kettle she turned, running an awkward hand through her ruffled hair.

'Do you want a top-up?'

Dave glanced at his almost empty mug. 'You know, I will have another wee cup, thank you.'

'So, you're up early.' She rinsed his mug briskly in the sink.

'Ah, it's Mattie, he woke me,' he replied, a little distracted.

'Really?' Susan said. 'That's strange, it's normally a battle in the morning to get him out of bed. Maybe today, for a change, he'll be in school on time.'

'Don't count on it,' said Dave, 'he's gone back to his room. I'd say he's out for the count.'

'He was probably all excited to have you back home again. It's been a long time for him.'

'It really sank in last night, just how long it's been.' Dave gazed at Susan. 'I couldn't get to sleep for hours: my mind was working overtime.' He sighed, feeling again how empty his bed had been, how lonely the room, and how the shadows on the walls had played havoc with his mind.

'It's only to be expected, I suppose.' Susan placed a fresh coffee in front of Dave. 'The last time you slept in there, you had June with you.' She stood still for a moment, reflecting. Then she sat down sadly at the table beside him. 'It couldn't have gone any worse really, could it?'

'No, you can say that again. I tried writing —' he urged her for confirmation — 'You know how many letters I sent here from England, don't you — at least a dozen!'

'At *least*.'

'She didn't answer. You didn't answer. You could have written, Susan. Told me she'd gone. Told me where to find her. *And* I'd given up the drink. You know, on the night that June left me, I smashed my last bottle of whiskey on the ground. That was the closest I ever got to getting on my hands and knees and licking it back up. I was in agony. But next morning I took a shower, then said to myself, *no more*. I wrote to June about it, in the first letter … and about the drink driving charges, and the two-month wait before the trial — and especially that I was sorry — But I heard nothing from her, of course. Two months off the booze, two months worrying about my trial — then the minute I was let off with a warning, I packed my bags and jumped on the first ferry back to Ireland …'

Susan's eyes were filled with deep sorrow. 'And I told you what had happened. And that's when you started drinking again.'

Dave let out a deep sigh, and changed the subject. 'Anyway, it's done. Let's talk about it later. So, what about you, how have you been?'

Susan reached for a cigarette and struck a match. 'Believe it or not, hardly anything has happened for me since then.'

'Have you been going out much, are you seeing anyone?' Dave was genuinely concerned.

'Dave, playing babysitter to your son doesn't leave a whole lot of time for a social life.' But the contempt in her voice shocked even her, especially when the guilt came to Dave's face. 'Sorry. Bygones be bygones, I suppose. And anyway, that's not all there is to it. I haven't had a desire to go out anywhere. I lost my inspiration.'

'But you used to love going out on the town, Susan; you always had that wee wild streak in you.'

Susan smiled bashfully.

'I know I did,' she said more brightly. 'But I'm getting old now, I've got to get serious at some point.' She frowned. 'To be honest, when you guys left for England and I started renting this place, everything kind of changed. I think I'd lived with Dad too long: he's the narkiest man ever but God knows I had it easy there. No rent, no bills — I hope he has me in his will, I'd love that place!' She laughed.

'How is he?'

'He's fit as a fiddle and doing his special bit to make everybody's life a living hell. I swear to God, since Mam left him he's turned into a mental case. He's always got his pet hates, his little missions to set things straight. He's forever writing complaint letters to this person and to that — and believe me, you better watch yourself, too.'

'Why?'

Susan looked shocked. 'Why? Are you serious?' He was. 'Because he hates your guts. As soon as he finds out that you're back home, he'll go after you.'

Dave sat back in his seat. 'Susan, he's got nothing to gain by going after me. I'm not the man I used to be.'

Susan made no comment; she didn't want to judge him.

'I know six weeks isn't that long off the drink,' Dave went on. 'I've been off it for longer in the past, but this time it's different, this time it's definitely for real.'

'It's not me you have to convince, Dave.' There was uncertainty in her voice. It was her turn to talk about something different: 'Mattie's really picked up at school.'

'Has he?' Dave was pleased. 'That's fantastic.'

'Yea, he's really started to concentrate more in his classes, and he's even telling me how much he loves different subjects, especially English. His teachers say he's got a great imagination.'

Dave smiled proudly. 'That's great to hear, especially considering everything that he's gone through.'

'I know.' Susan rose from the table and threw the cigarette butt into the bin.

'This morning ...' Dave hesitated — 'Mattie told me that June had been here.'

Susan looked back at him. 'I told you that he'd been seeing her, didn't I?' He's been telling me how she's walking him to school, and of how she tells him this and that.'

Dave stood up and walked distractedly to the back door, opening it briefly and then closing it again. He was trying to find the right words to say, but was at a loss.

'Honestly, Dave.' She spoke softly and with sorrow in her voice. 'I would give the world to see June walking through that back door, but she can't. You need to talk to Mattie and snap him out of this, and you need to make sure you don't get sucked in by the things he's saying. God knows I did and it just makes everything more difficult.'

Dave shrugged his shoulders reluctantly. 'I'll see how the next few days go. I'll listen to what he says ...'

Susan threw her hands in the air with annoyance. 'Don't be a fool, Dave. You are responsible for Mattie and his happiness. Do not indulge him in this. You're not going to find June in this house or anywhere near it. If you want to see her, drive up to Mayo like a normal person. And take Mattie while you're at it. He needs to accept that things have changed for your family.'

'Somebody's got a sleepy head.' Dave was alone in the kitchen when his son came in soon after. Don't mention the tantrum before, he thought. Mattie stopped to yawn, before sitting on the edge of Susan's chair. His eyes were still getting used to daylight and he rubbed at them sleepily.

His son was a good-looking boy. He had a gentle, inviting face with pronounced cheek- and jaw-lines, and when he smiled it often looked larger than life. He had an endearing quality. But of all his features, none could match the sparkle of his brilliantly blue eyes. Their intensity in his pale face was hypnotic. Strangers had been known to stop to look at him, and say, 'He'll be a heartbreaker that one.'

'No wonder you're tired,' said Dave, opening the cupboard. 'Sounds like you didn't sleep much last night.' Dave produced a white bowl and a spoon and placed them on the table in front of Mattie, who continued to yawn.

'Cover your mouth,' instructed Dave — startling himself with this instant return of fatherly behaviour. 'What would you like, corn flakes or porridge?'

'Corn flakes,' grumbled the boy tiredly. Dave filled the bowl with cereal and milk. Mattie dragged his chair closer and, after a moment's contemplation, shovelled a large spoonful into his mouth. Dave sat down alongside him.

'So how *did* you sleep?' quizzed Dave.

'Good, I think.' He deliberated for a second. 'But I woke up really early and went out with Mam. We chatted about you being home so I stayed awake for a while more.' Mattie glanced at his father.

Dave nodded and then casually continued, 'So Mammy was chatting with you, was she?'

'You know she was. I told you before.' Mattie smiled.

'Ah yea, silly me, I must be still tired myself.' Dave drank the remains of his coffee that had started to get cold and unsatisfying. He flinched. 'I better get another cup. You finish breakfast and we'll get ready for school.'

Mattie seemed distracted by the back of the corn flakes box, where details of free collectable football cards were displayed in brilliant colours.

'Did you hear me?'

'I did,' acknowledged Mattie, without looking at his father.

Looking at him, Dave heard June's voice in his head: 'Where has my baby boy gone?'

In the six months that had passed, particularly those first two before he could return to Ireland, Dave had had plenty of time to think and reflect. Often he'd spend hours at a time daydreaming about his wife and his son and the years that had led him to this point. It occurred to him during one of these deep reflections that he barely knew the nine-year-old Mattie, and that whenever he thought of him it was almost always as an infant. The drinking had certainly played its part in disconnecting him from family life: being drunk from Friday through to Sunday, and hungover for two days after, never left much quality time to spend with his son. Dave grimaced. He hated himself for his failures as a father, as a human being.

Mattie had become a part of June and Dave's life only three months after they'd married.

'I keep getting sick,' June had exclaimed one afternoon.

'So, do you really think you might be pregnant?' Dave was excited.

June regarded him with amusement. 'Look at you, the proud father already. I'll pop down to the doctor's tomorrow and find out.'

'I'll get off from work and we'll go down together!'

June smiled and nodded. She knew she was pregnant: she rarely got sick, and she could sense the change in her body and also to her mind.

The next day the result confirmed it, and June was elated, though she grimaced at the thought of the months ahead and labour. Dave was beside himself with joy. He threw his arms around her while she was still lying back on the cold surface of the practitioner's bed.

'Oh my God,' he whispered into her ear, 'this is the greatest news in the world!'

'I never knew that you were so clucky,' she said, kissing him on the cheek. 'You never let on that you wanted so much to be a father.'

'Are you joking me, I love children, I've always wanted to be a father — and you are going to be the sexiest mamma in town.'

The months that had followed were some of the most glorious for the newlyweds. Dave, who didn't drink as much back then, drank even less: his desires had diminished. And June was one of the lucky ones and didn't have much morning sickness.

It was a time of wonder and of planning, a time of the growing tummy and 'the baby's kicking!'. As the days flew by and the birth drew closer, theories of the child's sex started to emerge around them.

'If she waddles like a duck when she walks then it's definitely a boy.' One of Dave's drinking buddies who had five children of his own was quick with this.

'Waddles like a duck!' exclaimed Dave. 'What a load of rubbish.'

'It's *true*,' continued the friend. 'Watch June when she walks past you, if she sways from side to side, she's having a boy.'

Dave skolled his beer and rose to go home. Turning to his friend, he declared, 'You're full of shit, Seamus,' and laughed as he headed for the door.

'And if she's fat in the face,' Seamus shouted after him, 'she's having a girl — it's the hormones, it does crazy things to their weight distribution!'

Later that evening, after June had walked past him a few times as she pottered about the caravan, Seamus's theories came back into Dave's head.

'June, I'm going to make a prediction.'

June turned, curious.

'About what?'

'I'm predicting now, with a hundred per cent certainty, that you're having a boy.'

'Oh, really?' June placed her hands lovingly upon her large tummy, caressing it as she spoke. 'Well, I think you're wrong.' She lifted her T-shirt 'I had a dream last night that I had a girl, a gorgeous little girl. I'm convinced about it.'

'Oh no. No,' Dave said with absolute assurance, 'believe me, it's a boy.'

June eyed her husband suspiciously. 'You sound pretty certain there, Dave.'

He looked away with a childish grin on his face.

'What are you smiling at?' she asked. 'Is it because of this?' Suddenly June leant over slightly, stuck her bum out and flexed her arms in a winglike fashion. 'Quack, quack,' she bellowed as she began to prance around the space like a duck. 'Quack, quack!'

Dave smiled, embarrassed, like a trickster caught in the act. 'Ha-ha, very funny,' he cried.

June stopped and suddenly approached him. 'Are you saying I walk like a duck?' she teased, quacking again at the top of her lungs.

'No!' Dave could hardly contain himself — she was looking hilarious. 'No, you're more like a little chick, a hot chick!' Reaching out, he threw his arms around her waist and dragged her towards him. 'Come here, you crazy Daisy Duck you.' Just as he drew June in, he stopped suddenly: her eyes had opened wide with fright.

'Oh no!' she cried.

'Oh no is right,' exclaimed Dave as his eyes darted down her legs to the floor, where a puddle of water was spreading. 'By the look of that pond, we're going to have a baby duck tonight.' June was horrified, and he tried to calm her. 'Don't worry, it's all going to be fine. You stay here while I get your bag and then we'll head to the hospital.'

'Hurry!'

June's labour came on quite rapidly. Almost immediately she was in agonising pain. And when they arrived at the hospital, she was almost fully dilated. Only two hours later Matthew Stephen Finch arrived in the world with a barrage of cries. At nearly four kilograms, and fifty-four centimetres long, he was a large baby.

June lay beneath white hospital bedsheets, her face slack with exhaustion but, at the same time, filled with overwhelming triumph. Mattie was asleep, his pink wrinkled body curled up on her belly as though he was still in her womb, his eyes tightly closed. Dave sat on the edge of the bed, utterly emotional, his eyes still wet. He looked away briefly and then suddenly back again: it was so hard to comprehend the little life at June's breast.

'It's just incredible,' sighed June, taking her eyes from her son for the minutest of moments. 'Isn't he the most gorgeous little guy you have ever seen?'

Dave had seen the newborn babies of friends or relatives, and heard people speaking of how handsome a child was or how pretty its little head was. But he'd struggled to appreciate what they were seeing: through his eyes each was a baby not so different from another, with a cone-shaped head and dry flaky skin. He'd even once remarked in private to June, of a friend's baby, that it kind of resembled a little hamster.

Now, on the day that Mattie was born, Dave saw for the first time what all those parents before him had seen in their newborns, the unfathomable life that he and June had created. The life whose uniqueness alone was more brilliant than anything you might call *handsome* or *pretty* — in many respects it defined those words. Dave no longer saw the shape of the baby's head or the trauma to his skin; he only saw a little person who he knew he would love unconditionally for the rest of his life.

'I've never seen anything more beautiful,' replied Dave in a whisper — and then, staring at June, 'except, of course, his mother.'

'Wow, he's massive!' Susan had exclaimed, when she saw Mattie for the first time. Amazed, she looked at June, who was propped up in bed reading a magazine. 'Did you really push him out of you?'

June threw Susan an unimpressed but amused glance.

'Wow. You must have a huge fanny.'

'Susan!' cried June, appalled.

'Sorry … but he is big.'

It was true. Mattie had been very tall for a newborn, and would go on surprising people with his height and build.

'Oh, he's definitely going to be a basketball player when he grows up,' people would say when they discovered his age for the first time. Even Dave and June could be surprised by his stature sometimes.

'A, can you say the letter A?' Dave sat on the floor one day holding up handwritten pieces of paper in front of his boy. Mattie, two years old and three foot tall, eyed the paper and, after a moment's thought, he replied, 'Seven.' He turned away from Dave and began to play with his toy cars.

'No,' said Dave. 'It's A, can you say A five times? A, A, A, A, A.'

Mattie continued to play with his cars, much to Dave's displeasure.

'Mattie,' he said sternly, 'put those cars away and look at me. It's learning time.' Mattie disregarded his father.

'Mattie.' Dave raised his voice, reaching out suddenly and snatching a car from his son's grasp. 'Learning time!'

Mattie began to cry and the sound alerted June, who was in the kitchen ironing. She walked into the room and found Dave hugging the youngster, wiping away his tears.

'Ah, Dave,' she sighed. 'He's only two.'

Dave looked up at June. 'So what? He needs to learn. The kids he was playing with over the weekend can write their names, they know all this stuff already!'

'Which kids are you talking about?' quizzed June.

'Liam's twins — whatever their names are, I can't remember.'

'Those kids are nearly four years old!' said June, shocked.

'What?' Dave could hardly believe it. 'They were not, Mattie looked older than them, for Christ's sake.'

'I'm telling you, Dave, those kids are over a year older than Mattie.' Mattie left his father's arms and began to play with his cars again. His tears had already passed and were replaced by a grin.

'Jeez.' Dave discarded his paper scraps. 'I really thought they were the same age.'

June reflected. 'That's not saying we shouldn't be teaching him ... but we can't get annoyed with him if he doesn't get it, he's still really only a baby.'

Mattie was quite an introverted child, more of an observer than a doer. With other kids, he'd rarely get involved in games at first; generally he would stand back and watch what was happening — he'd take it all in. And sometimes June could have moments of flawed judgement too.

'Go play with the other children,' she might urge from the park bench, a newspaper piled on her lap. But Mattie would continue to play alone, picking up dirt with his little plastic shovel or driving his Matchbox cars over imaginary dunes, all the time maintaining a studious eye on the activities of the other children.

'Mattie, why are you on your own?' June would press. 'Go over and say hello to the little boy!'

Only when he'd got some confidence from observing them, though, would Mattie pluck up the courage to join the others. Hauling himself up the small ladder to the top of the slide, unlike the other kids he wouldn't make the mistake of moving too fast along the ladder and slipping through the steps. And he could run across the shaky rope bridge with the uneven floor, having watched how to step down carefully onto the bridge.

'It's great,' Dave once observed, 'he's always ahead of his game, he doesn't make the same mistakes as those other kids.'

June looked doubtful. 'Playing it safe isn't a whole lot of fun — sometimes it's important to make mistakes: it's good for your character.'

Those early years of Mattie's life had been, for June and Dave, a time of overanalysing. As it turned out though, when there was nobody to learn from Mattie bullishly ran headlong into things just like every other child.

Still, he did spend a great deal of his time thinking about things. Sometimes at night, putting him to bed would be an ordeal, a battle of wills pitching endless protests against Dave or June's patience. Yet on most other nights there would be silence. Mattie would often lie awake for hours, staring at the ceiling, watching the shadows moving there, seemingly consumed in thought. June would stand unnoticed at his bedroom door, watching.

'Do you think there's something wrong with him?' she asked Dave one night. 'It's as though he goes into some kind of trance. What two-year-old does that?'

'Ah, June, I really don't know. We spend our time interpreting everything the little guy does — he's probably just got a very active imagination.' Dave smiled. 'He could be one of those gifted children!'

June laughed. 'Don't get your hopes up, I've seen him running around the house with a saucepan on his head.' Dave laughed, but June became concerned again. 'I just don't know, he seems to be lost in his own world sometimes. It's not just bedtime, he does this kind of thing during the day also.'

Dave hadn't noticed. 'Like what?'

'There've been days when he's playing away and having a great time and I'll leave the room for a second, and when I come back in he'll just be standing there like a statue, looking at something.'

Dave was puzzled. 'Just staring at something?'

'Yea. And then I'll approach him and he'll suddenly look up at me like nothing's been happening and start playing again.'

'That's weird.'

'Too right it's weird. And —' she hesitated before continuing — 'this probably sounds completely ridiculous, but one time I'm nearly positive I saw him waving at something in the living room.'

'Ah, June — what are you saying?'

'Well, I don't know, maybe he has an imaginary friend; it was so freaky.'

Dave wasn't convinced. 'It's strange all right, but honestly, I think it's an overactive imagination. At his age, if he's got an active mind, it'd be hard for him to know what's real and what's not.'

'You think so?' She was upset.

'I'm sure of it.'

Dave seemed to be correct. Growing up, going to pre-school, Mattie had become more occupied, and his trances became a thing of the past. It wasn't until he was five that June's suspicions were roused again.

'I'm serious, Dave,' she said one evening, sounding a little tense. 'I heard him say it.'

'What was he doing when he said it?'

June spoke slowly. 'He was sitting in the front room watching television.'

Dave tried to make some sense of what she was saying. 'So you walked into the room, tidied up a bit and then, just as you were about to leave, he said it?'

'Yea.' She softened her voice. 'As clear as day. I was walking out of the room and without it being any big deal at all he just suddenly said, "Hi, Charlie!"'

'And are you sure he said *Charlie*?'

'I'm positive,' persisted June, gesturing. 'I looked back at him and he was staring past me into the hallway.'

Dave went silent as he gathered his thoughts.

'Dave.' June spoke softly. 'Uncle Charlie died three months ago.'

Dave was serious. 'He must have heard us talking about him ... Have we mentioned Charlie lately?'

June nodded.

'Then Mattie's being a little shit!' Dave was getting angry. 'Where is he now?'

'He's up in his bedroom.'

'I'm going to have a talk with him.'

Dave sprang to his feet and stormed upstairs.

'Mattie, I want to speak to you.'

The youngster turned around on his bed, where he'd been lying in a sulk ever since he'd been sent to his room.

'I didn't do anything wrong, Daddy, I promise!'

Dave looked at his son's sad eyes, and held his gaze. 'Your mammy is very upset, she said you were talking about her uncle Charlie.'

Mattie bit his lower lip nervously. 'I just said hello to Uncle Charlie.'

Dave sat down on the bed alongside him. 'But, Mattie, you know it's not very nice to play tricks on people, don't you?'

'But I didn't play a trick, Daddy — I saw Uncle Charlie and I said hello.'

Dave's eyes narrowed. 'You saw Uncle Charlie?'

Mattie turned quickly, burying his head in the pillow. 'I was being good.'

'Mattie, turn around to me. Are you saying for sure that you saw Uncle Charlie?'

Mattie faced Dave. 'I was being good!' With that he returned to his pillow, and became unreachable.

Dave persisted, without success.

But later that evening, Mattie entered the living room where June sat alone.

'Sorry, Mammy, for playing a trick. I won't talk to Charlie again!' He had sincere regret on his face, and June embraced him warmly.

Now, years later in this same house after so much had passed, Susan arrived back in the kitchen to find Dave once again sitting alone. She was still in her dressing gown, and a newly lit cigarette burned in her right hand. She was disgruntled.

'Did Mattie eat all of his breakfast?'

'I think he was more interested in the free football cards than the cereal, but he did all right.'

'Is he getting ready for school?'

'Yes,' replied Dave. 'I'm going to walk him, on my way — I've got an interview.'

She couldn't maintain small talk for much longer. 'Dave, for heaven's sake, watch yourself with June: Mattie *isn't* talking to her. He wants to, but he can't. Believe me, for a time there I contemplated moving to my mam's in Mayo so that he could be closer to June, but what use would that be?' She became saddened. 'You're not long off the drink, I would hate to see you going back onto it — that's the last thing that any of us need right now.'

Dave sighed. 'Don't worry, Susan. I know you're just looking out for me. I'll be all right.'

Mattie's feet pounding down the stairs signalled Dave to make a move. He gave Susan a quick kiss on the cheek. 'It's really great to be home and thanks for everything. It's going to be fine.'

As Dave disappeared from the room Susan took a drag on her cigarette and whispered, 'I hope you know what you're doing,' before turning on the radio and making a start to her day.

Moments later the front door closed and Dave and Mattie set off up the street together.

'You know we nearly ended up living there.' Dave pointed towards one of the more up-market estates along the road to school.

'I know,' replied Mattie. 'Mam tells me that all the time.'

'Does she?'

'Yea, every time she walks me to school.'

Dave felt a lot older today, as though a lifetime had passed since he'd last taken this trek. The early morning traffic was beginning to back up. Dave looked at his watch: it was half past eight.

'When did she last walk you to school?' Dave asked after a few moments of silence.

'Yesterday.' Mattie stopped suddenly and turned to Dave. 'Are you home for good, Dad, or will you be leaving again?'

Dave was caught by surprise. 'For good, Mattie, absolutely for good.'

Mattie was still bothered. 'Will you be drinking?'

Dave's face dropped. 'No, Mattie, I'm finished with it. I promise you I will never put another drink to my lips.'

'I'm happy about that,' replied the boy; he seemed to mature more with every sentence he spoke. 'Because I hate you when you're drunk!' Mattie turned away like an insect that's just stung its prey.

'You hate me when I'm drunk?' Dave rested a hand gently on his son's shoulder, bringing his attention back. Mattie eyed his father. There was a coolness in those eyes that Dave had never seen before.

'Yes,' he replied, his gaze poisonous now. Mattie set off again, and Dave caught up. He was torn inside, his spirit ripped open.

'Good morning, Mattie!' waved Terry, cheerily directing traffic at the school crossing.

'And Dave,' he acknowledged when he'd brought them safely across the road. 'I haven't seen you in ages.'

'I've been away,' replied Dave carefully, 'working.'

'Ah, very good.' Terry glanced at the traffic. 'And Mrs Finch.' He turned to Mattie. 'Is your mother about today?'

Dave's heart froze. 'You've seen June?' he said uncertainly.

'Of course I have.' Terry kept his eyes fixed on Dave's and spoke in a light tone. 'I see her most days, don't I, Mattie?'

Mattie had disconnected himself from the conversation, having seen his friend Niall in the distance. 'I better go in,' he exclaimed, 'I want to hang out with Niall!'

Dave turned to his son. 'Okay, you take it easy and I'll see you tonight.' He was a little rattled. Terry was just playing along, right?

With that, Mattie dashed off into the school. Terry had already returned to his task. Dave took the opportunity to cross back, and checked his watch. He'd have to hurry to get to the interview at the factory on time.

It had all happened so suddenly. Stephen was driving erratically, the knuckles of his right hand hurting from the terrible punch he'd given his older brother. The road ahead was nothing more than a mish-mash of shapes and colours that slipped by him at speed — and the only thing that Stephen could see was the image of his brother Dave lying collapsed on the footpath. The car radio continued to hum but the voice in Stephen's head was June's: 'Come back, help your brother; you need to come back!'

'What was I thinking?' snarled Stephen, belting the steering wheel. His mind filled with memories of growing up in Belfast and of his older brother, who had protected him and watched out for him. Almost like the blinking of an eye, their years of childhood wonderment and games had come and gone so fast that it was hard to believe they'd ever happened at all.

Had Stephen always been so violently jealous? Was he born with that flaw in his character? And was it a foregone conclusion that in the future this flaw would ruin not just his life but the lives of the people he loved most?

'Everybody has their demons,' his father had once said to him. 'There isn't a person alive who's perfect. All we can do is try to control our flaws; never let them get the better of us.'

Stephen was born with a fire in his belly: from the moment of his first shrill cry, he had expressed impetuousness and determination. He had love for others, but a greater love for his own opinions, and with that came an iron-clad shell of pride.

'And that's your demon,' continued his father. 'Pride.'

'That's ridiculous!'

'It's not,' replied his father. 'I see you, you can be so hot-headed when it comes to things that you feel proud of. Pride in your family, pride in your country and most of all, pride in yourself. It can blind you, Stephen, it can make you do crazy things. It can make you jealous and vicious all in one.'

Stephen reflected on those words now, as he drove away from his injured brother. He hadn't spoken to his father for months after that conversation: again his pride got the better of him. When they finally did speak again, it was clear to both father and son that their relationship, previously strong and truthful, had been irreversibly damaged — and replaced with brief sentences spoken more out of necessity than anything else. And when his father was found dead, it tore Stephen to shreds.

'What a dickhead I am,' he moaned over the steering wheel, his voice cold. 'What if I've killed Dave?' He was back in the countryside, the car only moments from Johnny's house. What should I do? he thought remorsefully — hide his head and hope by some miracle, some divine intervention, everything would work its way back to how it had been, before jealousy and hatred had filled his body with poison?

'He's dead,' said Stephen, his eyes brimming with tears as he slammed on the brakes outside the house. He sat in the car sobbing. He could visualise the blood spilling onto the pavement from Dave's head, the life being stolen from those bright eyes. Mopping his face with the sleeve of his shirt, Stephen fought to pull himself up from the depths. There was little to comfort him now, as bewilderment, and self-pity invaded his mind: 'He's definitely dead, I killed my own brother.'

Then a tap on the car window broke into his nervous melancholy.'

Much to June's amazement, Dave came around, his eyes snapping open in fright.

Seeing June staring at him though, his fear retreated, and he felt happiness seeping in.

'Oh, thank you, God, thank you so much!' June spoke to the heavens and then carefully kissed Dave on the cheeks. His first instinct was to stand, but his fumbling fingers discovered the wound on the back of his head. He decided that it was best to stay put.

'The ambulance is on its way, can you hear it?' June was shaking, her beautiful face had been stripped of its glow, leaving strain and confusion. A chaotic spiral of sounds grew louder with each second, as the ambulance careened along the road to Stonebridge.

'I feel like I've been hit by a jackhammer,' said Dave dazedly. He winced as pain coursed from the back of his head. Then he tried to rise again —

'You need to stay where you are,' cried June, glaring into his face.

'But what about Stephen?'

'What about him?' snapped June. 'The police will be looking for him now.'

'The police!' Dave was suddenly awake. 'You called the police?' He began to struggle against the stabbing pain, trying to lift himself from the pavement.

'Dave, you've got to stay lying down, you can't move until the ambulance gets here!' June tried to hold him still but he battled to a seated position. Blood rushed from the cut in his head.

'We can't call the police for Stephen. I've got to go and warn him — I've got to protect him!'

June gasped, her eyebrows rising. 'Dave, are you insane, he tried to kill you! I nearly lost you. Leave this for the police.'

'*No.*' Dave rose to his feet, pressing the palm of his hand against the back of his head. It had all come back to him now. 'You don't understand, he's in danger, I can't leave it like this —'

The ambulance turned into the cul-de-sac. Seeing it arrive, the neighbours retreated indoors, spying through the curtains of their front-room windows.

'The ambulance is here. You can't go anywhere.'

Dave could barely stand. He felt the pressure from his head dragging him back to the ground and he wavered unsteadily. June had a comforting hold on him.

Two men in white medical gear shot out of the ambulance. June quickly explained what had happened.

'I have to go,' said Dave impatiently.

'I don't think you have much of a choice.' The older of the two medics had his hands on Dave's head. 'That's a nasty cut you have on the back of your head here.'

'Can't you just bandage it up? I'm feeling all right.'

'Dave, do what you're told, or you'll end up collapsing into a ditch if you're not lucky.' June was suddenly angry. Was he not concerned over his wellbeing? Or hers? And how could he want to protect the brother who'd caused him such harm?

The medic finished examining Dave's head: 'It's quite a cut … plenty of blood. But you're lucky, it's not as serious as it looks.' He ran Dave through a series of standard questions and checked his eyes.

June frowned. 'Will he have to go to hospital?' She felt hopeful that he would — at least then he'd avoid another confrontation with his brother.

The medic checked the gash again. He'd managed to stop the bleeding now and he shook his head. 'No,' he replied chirpily. 'He doesn't have concussion, though he'll be a bit groggy for a while, and we'll put on a good strong bandage so he doesn't need stitches. It will do till tomorrow — visit your GP then and he'll dress it again.'

Dave could see the disappointment on June's face. 'June, I have to see him, it's going to be all right.'

'How do you know?' she replied vehemently. 'How do you know he's not waiting back at Johnny's to finish you off as soon as you walk through the front door?'

The two medics listened in as they swabbed the wound and began to apply the bandage.

'He won't, June,' Dave said irritably, 'he's my brother!'

June shook her head in disgust. 'Your brother, eh? Did you think that your brother could do *this* to you? Did you think your brother could get so jealous that he'd waylay you with a punch and then — seeing you unconscious on the ground, maybe even dead — he would get into his car and drive off!'

This came as news to Dave: 'He saw me unconscious?'

'Yes, he saw you unconscious. He ran as soon as the blood appeared. I was screaming my guts out for him to come back but he just sped away down the road!'

Dave was puzzled. 'I had it in my head that he hit me and then ran ... that he didn't mean to hurt me as bad as he did. But he saw that I was badly injured, and he just ran away?'

'Like a coward, like a spineless coward.' June saw the opportunity here: 'So leave it for the police. Stephen's dangerous. I know you love your brother, but he's not himself today.'

The older medic felt he had to comment. 'Best do

what she's telling you, lad,' he said as he fastened the bandage. 'It looks and sounds to me like a job for the police.'

Dave shrugged at this, but he was uneasy. 'I can't believe that he would do that ... but I've still got to see him.' With the bandage firm around his head, Dave felt he was regaining control of his faculties, and the tugging weight had been lifted.

'Keep that on until you see the doctor. He'll check you over.'

The medics packed up, shook June's hand and left.

Dave turned to June. 'I've got to go,' he said. 'I've got to make things right.'

They say that you can never outrun your past, and Stephen was confronted with that as the tears dried on his face. He expected the tap on his window to be the police — hunting him down for the slaying of his older brother. But it wasn't the police.

The gentle tap was followed by a powerful blow and the windscreen disappeared before Stephen's eyes. He scrambled for cover inside the car. Shattered glass poured around him and figures appeared in the night air.

Just as Stephen lunged desperately for the back seat, a steel bar powered in and ravaged his exposed back. Knifing into his upper spine, it paralysed him with pain.

'Get out, you fucking bollix!' a harsh Northern accent barked from the darkness. Another swipe from the metal bar connected with Stephen's shoulderblade.

If he could just reach the back seat, get some time to collect himself, to get prepared —

'You've got nowhere to hide, Stephen,' the voice boomed, and the car door suddenly opened. Stephen recoiled as the metal bar was thrust at his legs, hammering at his feet in a flurry. Then hands grabbed hold of his ankles and began tugging.

Stephen's heart thundered crazily; he knew that he was without hope. He tried to grab onto anything within reach — but he landed face first on the stony roadside anyway, at the feet of three men.

'Mick,' he cried in desperation to the man who'd been doing all the talking. 'I'm sorry about your son, I didn't mean to get him stitched up for this. I was frightened.' He lay in a heap on the ground, body aching. 'I knew I'd get caught if I crossed the border with that stuff in the car!'

Mick Macklin was a tall, thin, razor-nosed man with greasy hair and greying stubble on his face. His looks fitted: indiscriminate but at the same time weasel-like, he could shake a man's hand as easily as cut it off. 'Shut your gob, Stephen!' he commanded, staring at him in an intense, haggard way.

Stephen became quiet, glancing at the faces of the three men. He didn't know the other two, but he was terrifyingly sure of the iron bars they were brandishing.

'Stephen, do you think I like doing this?' Mick offered him a fake smile of commiseration. 'I don't. The Lord knows I have better things to be doing than chasing after your sorry bollix down South.'

Stephen looked at him with wide eyes.

'But,' continued Mick with a sigh, 'the fact of the matter is that my son is now going to prison.' He raised his eyebrows and Stephen saw the starkness of his face. 'On top of that, I have cops knocking at my door, asking me questions.'

'I'm sorry about that, Mick, honestly —'

Mick's shoe ploughed through to his crotch, sending him rolling.

'Shut your fucking gob!' he yelled fiercely. Then he calmly continued, 'The bottom line, Stephen, is that I have no choice. I have to kill you. Not just for me but for the pride of my family. Do you understand?'

'You don't *have* to,' pleaded Stephen. 'I'll go back up North, I'll admit to the police that I was driving, that I'm to blame.'

Mick glanced at the two men, and then turned away from Stephen.

'Honestly, Mick, I'm sorry.' There was utter desperation in Stephen's voice, as he watched Mick walk away and get into a black car nearby.

Mick's two men approached Stephen. His breath came in quick, desperate gasps. 'Please,' he begged, 'please don't do this! Help! Help me —' An iron bar smashed into his face, snapping his jawbone. Cradling his body and covering his face, Stephen tried to protect himself. But through the cloud of fists and iron bars came the single thought, *Please let it end soon.* In the end, his body became limp and he could no longer hold on. As he lay motionless, feeling the remainder of his life slipping away, Stephen became aware that the men had stopped and were looking down at him.

Were they going to leave him? Stephen thought about Dave — maybe he was all right! And maybe they'd have a chance to make things right. Stephen could say that he was sorry.

One of the men crouched down and looked into his eyes.

'Sorry for your trouble, Stephen.' He was old, shaven-headed, possibly in his sixties. 'This last one is from me: its a message for your brother, David.' The man rose to his feet and Stephen looked up and saw him get a firmer grip on the iron bar. There was a scar deep in the centre of his wrist, the reminder of a wound caused when a knife had been plunged right through.

Then the iron bar landed, and Stephen was gone.

Johnny's house was just over four miles from Stonebridge, which in a car could be done in fifteen minutes, but on foot would be closer to one hour, since the narrow country roads were hilly and winding.

Dave wasn't able to hitch a lift.

He thought at first that the bandage on his head would attract sympathy from passing motorists, but it seemed to have the opposite effect. As cars whizzed by, the faces of drivers and passengers looked uncertain and worried. Dave imagined the conversations in the cars: 'It's probably from a bar fight' Or, 'You'd never know what illness he has.'

So Dave started off walking. There was no footpath and the narrowness of the road left only a scratch of earth bordering the hedges on either side. Cars flew around the bends, forcing him to duck and weave along this lumpy strip.

Dave pressed a hand to the back of his head. The throbbing pain had returned, and his cheek was swollen and tender where Stephen's punch had made contact.

As he walked, Dave struggled to deal with the notion that his brother could leave him for dead. He thought about his relationship with June, the instant romance that had sparked this chaos. It wasn't wrong that he loved her so suddenly; it wasn't foolish of him to keep their relationship a secret from Stephen — was it?

There was nothing going on between Stephen and her, anyway, he thought. So why hadn't he told Stephen?

The truth of the matter was that Dave had known from the outset that his brother wouldn't be able to handle it. Pride! Even when we were growing up it was the same bullshit, he thought wretchedly.

Dave tried to ignore his tiredness, which was growing with each step. He thought instead of Stephen as a teenager, and remembered how hot-headed he was. Francie and Dave would avoid talking to Stephen on topics which they knew he had strong feelings about.

'You need to control your temper,' Dave had once said in a firm voice, aware that this very topic of conversation could spark an argument. 'It's almost getting to the stage where we can't talk to you at all without you biting our heads off.'

Stephen hadn't answered. He just threw an exasperated glance at his brother and left the room.

There were times when Dave almost hated Stephen, when he could barely stand to see his brother's face. During those periods, it often felt like the world was an easier place to live, less chaotic, less under threat — but at the same time, it lacked spark. And it was this — Stephen's energy — that kept Francie and Dave coming back: it forever re-energised their spirits to forgive him one more time, to start over again.

In Dave's mind, as his feet began to weigh heavy on the road towards Johnny's house, everything was like old times again: Stephen had hurt him but Dave was chasing after him to accept his apology. Was Dave being ridiculous?

One thing Dave knew about himself for certain was that when it came to his family, he had a way of always remembering their positive traits. Whenever he thought of Stephen, he saw the man who could keep a crowd of people engrossed as he told stories of his life or cracked one of his endless supply of jokes. He thought about the man who at six o'clock every morning after their father's death would visit his graveside and talk to the man as though he stood beside him. Dave rarely thought about Stephen's anger. If he closed his eyes he could hear his loud expressive laugh; he would see him loaning Francie money, despite it being his last ten bob. If he thought hard enough he would remember the conversations he'd have with his brother when they discussed their lives and how they both wanted to leave Ireland for good and travel the world. He would remember that within the hard shell there existed a man who wanted more from his life.

'Time fairly flies by,' Stephen had said only a few mornings before at Johnny's house.

'You can say that again,' agreed Dave, with a thoughtful frown.

'Pretty soon we'll just be two old men, the same as all those old codgers you find in the pubs with their pints of Guinness and their pipes.' He'd paused and then continued, absently, 'We'd want to make something of our lives soon, because before we know it, we'll be gone!'

He's not a bad man, Dave was musing when finally he reached the lane that led up to Johnny's house, just a bit confused.

The tree-lined laneway was one continuous bend. It wasn't until the house was only metres away that Dave caught sight of Stephen.

'*Oh Jesus Christ, no!*' he yelled and broke into a terrible sprint, hurling himself to his brother.

'Oh, what have they done to you?' cried Dave, his temples pounding thickly, his throat tight. Was he still breathing, was there any hope? But as he leant down to help Stephen breathe, to find his heart, he realised that it was all over.

Stephen was cool and appallingly still.

'Christ!' he called out to the heavens, uncontrollably distressed. 'How could you fucking do this? How could you?'

He raised Stephen's lifeless body into his arms and tried to wipe away the blood but the face that lay beneath no longer looked like Stephen, it had been mangled, every bone shattered.

Dave's tears fell burning from his eyes. The pain ran through every inch of his body and he felt more agony than any physical injury, any wound, could ever inflict on him.

'What's happened?' Johnny suddenly came running from inside the house. Reaching Dave, he jumped back in horror. Stephen lay bloody across Dave's lap.

'They've taken him,' wept Dave. 'The bastards have killed my brother.'

Johnny reeled, stunned and stricken. He went pale and sat down abruptly.

Dave glanced at him and then back to his brother. 'Look at him, Johnny, I can't even recognise his face, they've mutilated him!'

Johnny looked away, it was too difficult to take in.

'Don't fucking sit there, call the police!' Dave couldn't contain himself suddenly. Johnny stood and started towards the house.

'Where were you?' screamed Dave, realising how little help the police would be.

Johnny stopped and after a moment turned to face Dave. 'I was here all day,' he sobbed. 'I've been asleep.'

Dave wiped tears from his eyes. All the will had been drained out of him but still Johnny's revelation hit him hard. 'You *slept* through this?' He held Stephen higher. 'You slept soundly while Stephen got this sort of beating right outside your fucking bedroom window?' Dave placed his brother gently upon the ground and rose to his feet, deadly earnest.

Johnny was instantly terrified. 'I took sleeping pills, there was nothing I could do, I didn't *know*.'

Dave ran towards him, fists clenched, intent on lashing out at Johnny but as soon as he reached the smaller, petrified man, he halted. There was nothing to fight for any more.

'I'm sorry, Dave, I'm really sorry!'

Dave fell into a desperate embrace with Johnny, and seconds later he passed out. The world went black, there was nothing left.

The funeral was in Belfast five days later; Stephen's casket was lowered into his father's grave. It seemed that the world and its mother had turned out to see Stephen off and Dave took some comfort in knowing that his brother had left a positive mark on so many lives. There were also many unfamiliar faces in the crowd and the heavy police presence confirmed a paramilitary attendance.

At the church Dave heard nothing; as he helped carry the casket to the graveside behind the lone bagpiper his mind was empty; and as he tried to comfort his mother and sister, he was numb.

Sorry for your troubles! He'd been hearing this all morning from mournful friends, who shook his hand and talked about their memories of Stephen's short life. What did that mean? As he stood in the chatter, he wrestled with the notion of what those troubles were. Did it mean the guilt that his mother would lay on him for not looking after her youngest son, for taking him away and getting him killed? Surely she knew about his 'secret' life? — but she'd find it easier to blame Dave than accept Stephen's culpability.

Perhaps his troubles would be the days of drinking that Dave could see coming — whiskey and beer against the loss of his brother and his separation from the woman he loved.

He would be stuck here; he would lose his job down South. 'Sorry for your troubles!' It was like a prediction of the future, the spiral of events that would follow the death.

*

Hours turned into days and pretty soon they became weeks.

'You can't stay here.'

The bar near home in Belfast was empty. It was the middle of the afternoon and Dave could hardly stand up; his body was arched over the counter with a glass of whiskey close by.

June's voice came as a shock. Dave turned suddenly, losing his footing — and landed on the floor with a thud.

The publican looked up at the sound, but June waved — 'I've got him!' — and she leant down over Dave.

'Are you all right, Dave?'

He was a mess on the floor.

'June?' The glow of her healthy face came into focus.

'Yes, Dave, it's me.' She spoke softly, almost dreamily.

'You look like an angel,' he said with a sudden laugh. 'What are you doing in Belfast?'

'I came to get you.' She placed her soft hand on his. 'I came to bring you back to Stonebridge.'

Dave looked away, ashamed of the tears that instantly welled in his eyes. 'Stephen is dead, June, he's dead.'

'I know, David, your sister Francie wrote me a letter … She said you were having a tough time.' She leant in next to Dave, who had begun to sob, and held his head close to her chest. 'I'm so sorry.' June's eyes filled too, but she contained herself, blinking and breathing deeply.

'I wish you had told me,' she continued in a low, calming voice. 'I wish I could have been there for you. I was worried sick. The last I saw of you was that afternoon. I didn't know what had happened till it was in the papers days later. You vanished without a word.'

Dave said nothing. He didn't want her presence to be clouded in drunken slurs and useless comments.

'Come on.' She helped him to his feet. 'Francie has packed your bag and I've got it in the car out front. Let's go.'

As the bar door swung closed and the blinding daylight hit Dave's eyes, he thought about his brother. 'I'm sorry, Stephen,' he whispered to himself. 'I'm leaving with her.'

June helped Dave into the car. Turning the ignition she glanced over at him. 'It's going to be all right, Dave, everything will be all right.'

He shut his eyes and June pulled away from the parking lot. Stonebridge was five hours away and she had no intention of stopping until she got there.

January 1990

'Have you got a girlfriend?'

Mattie was startled by his father's voice: he was still getting used to having him at home again.

'I didn't know you were there,' he replied, turning to the doorway where Dave was standing; he'd been watching him style his hair in the bathroom mirror.

'So, do you have a girlfriend?' repeated his father.

Mattie blushed. 'No!'

'Are you sure? By the amount of Brylcreem you're putting in your hair, I'd say you're trying to impress someone.' Dave shook his head in dour amusement. 'What does your mam think of your hair like this, does she like it?'

'Sometimes.' Mattie's eyes opened wide with excitement. 'She says it makes me look handsome!'

'Really?' Dave nodded and went to stand behind Mattie, both of them facing the mirror. 'You know, I think she's right. I've said it before and I'll say it again, you do look as handsome as your dad.'

Mattie turned swiftly, smiling. 'Not as you, she never said anything about you.'

With a lump in his throat, Dave turned away to hide his disappointment.

'She doesn't talk about me, eh?' he spoke quietly, embarrassed to be asking this of his young son.

'Nah.' Mattie was unaffected and still cheery. 'You should talk to her yourself, I don't know why you keep asking me so many questions.'

Two weeks had passed since Dave returned home, and for the first time it was just him and Mattie. Susan had decided to give them both space: she said they needed to rediscover each other.

'Where will you go?' asked Dave, on the day that she left.

'Believe it or not, back to my dad's,' she replied with a humourless smile.

'Are you mad?'

'I must be.' She carried her suitcase to the door. 'I'm not just doing this for Mattie, you know, I'm doing it for you too.'

Dave was puzzled. 'What do you mean?'

'I didn't want to tell you this because you've enough on your plate as it is, but I think it's best that you know.' There was concern in her voice. 'I heard through the grapevine that Dad has been talking to social welfare —'

'What?' Dave was instantly upset. 'Social welfare — what about? What's that nutcase up to now?'

Susan turned away. 'That's why I didn't want to mention it to you, I knew you'd react this way.'

Dave was still angry. 'Susan, of course I'd react this way. I'm not a bloody fool, I know what social welfare means!'

Susan frowned. 'You need to calm down or I can't talk to you about this.'

'Calm down —' Dave struggled, seeing the annoyance on Susan's face, then contained himself. 'I'm calm, don't worry, I'm calm. I just can't believe it.'

'Me too,' she said darkly. 'He's a bitter old man with too much time on his hands, and knowing you're back home has just put fuel onto his fire.'

Dave reflected. 'So what's he trying to get social welfare to do? Assess my ability as a father?'

'Worse,' she said regretfully. 'He wants them to take Mattie away from you, to give him to a relative or to social services.'

Dave took a deep, furious sigh. 'Are you serious?'

Susan softened her tone. 'Don't worry, it's all nonsense. Anyway, I'm going to spend some time with him, and as soon as he gets reminded what a failure I am in his eyes, he'll forget all about you and Mattie.' Susan smiled grimly. 'I'll wear a few low-cut tops — if they still fit me — and in no time he'll be so distracted with telling me how much of a slapper I am, he'll have forgotten all about you.'

Dave could see the hurt and sadness cross Susan's face. 'That's bullshit, Susan, and you know it.' He gave her a hug.

'Not to my father it's not.'

'Just don't go near him, Susan. Social services will find nothing on me, and we'll beat your dad at his own game!'

Susan shook her head, stepping back. 'Dave, trust me …' She paused. 'Dad is on every committee in town and he can be quite powerful if he wants to be. Honestly, I want to do this — I want to give you and Mattie a shot at getting things back on track. You two need some private time together.'

Dave had seen how well-connected Michael was, after years of befriending — and bullying — all sorts of powerful people, from parish priests to local members of parliament. He could be very dangerous.

'It'll work out for the best,' continued Susan. 'You just stay off the gargle and, for God's sake, give it a rest with the questions about June.'

'I haven't been asking any questions.'

Susan threw Dave a knowing look. 'We both know you have. Like I said before, talk to her yourself — that's fine — but stop using Mattie as some kind of go-between.'

Dave stood like a punished child. 'All right,' he replied with a sigh.

'Good,' concluded Susan. 'And I'll come back to see you both in a few weeks' time!'

As soon as Mattie had finished styling his hair, he went down to the kitchen and slung his schoolbag over his shoulder.

'You all set?' Dave was searching around. 'Have you seen my keys?'

Mattie stood still and it was his silence that made Dave glance at him. He looked awash with emptiness suddenly, as though something had died in him.

Dave came closer. 'What's wrong, Mattie, has something happened?'

'I was just thinking,' replied Mattie sullenly, staring at the floor.

Dave knelt down in front of the boy and raised his

head gently. 'What were you thinking about? What's got you feeling so sad all of a sudden?'

'You never said sorry to me.'

Dave was confused.

'What do you mean? Sorry for what?'

'When you hit me in the face, you never said you were sorry!'

Dave was shocked. 'Hit you in the face! When did I do that?'

'When we were in England. Do you not remember? It was just before Mammy and I came back home to Ireland.'

Dave abruptly had a glimpse of the past. It was a muddled, drunken image, hazed like the image left in your eyes from the blinding flash of a camera. Dave grew uncomfortable. He saw their living room in England, the matted grey carpet and the rented chest of drawers with the missing handles. He saw the bleakness of that room in darkness, only the light from the hallway streaking in. He could see himself, sitting on the floor with two half-drunk glasses of whiskey resting nearby. And then Mattie appeared, his eyes flooded with tears, their powerful blue clouded over with disbelief —

The memory disappeared.

'I think I remember.'

Mattie was angry: 'You don't remember, I can tell!'

Dave rested his hands comfortingly on his son's shoulders. He wished he *could* remember what had happened. But it was too difficult right now to collect his thoughts, to replay the memory and trudge through the haze to discover its beginning and its end.

Mattie shrugged his father's hands off. 'You never remember the things that you do!'

Dave was taken aback. He felt he had to turn the argument around. 'Mattie, where's all this coming from? Only minutes ago you were happy as Larry and now you're like a whole different kid.'

'I don't want to talk to you any more!' Mattie yelled at the top of his voice, storming out of the room.

'Mattie! Come back here this second, or —' But the front door slammed and Dave knew he had lost this battle. Mattie would be well and truly out of sight by now.

'What did I *do*?' He must have been drunk one night in England and *something* happened. He could still see Mattie's tear-filled eyes — but there was no memory of what had led to those tears.

I *must* have hit him, he thought. He wouldn't try one on like that.

He scratched his head, disappointed and frustrated. He felt a sudden longing for a drink.

'Alcohol is the last thing I need right now!' he growled at himself, angry. It had now been eight weeks since he last took a drink, but in recent days the desire had stirred in him again. Returning back home, the history contained within the walls of this house, Mattie's relationship with June, and how empty that was making Dave feel — all this and a soulless job at the factory, and the pressures from in-laws. He didn't know how he'd keep going if things didn't get better with Mattie.

But the boy had been different in the last few days.

When Dave first returned home, he hadn't sensed any animosity from him. The absence of his father didn't seem to have left scars and Mattie appeared genuinely thrilled to have Dave home. But as the first weekend at home came and went, a familiar longing crept in. Since he'd quit, he'd been writing in a diary every time he felt the desire to drink. Over the course of that first weekend at home, he made nine entries.

This is harder than I thought it would be. If there was a bottle of whiskey sitting in front of me now I'd find it nearly impossible not to drink it. But where would that lead me to — the rubbish heap! I'm not going to give in to this,

I'm a better man than that and I owe it to my family, I owe it to my son. I adore Mattie so much, he's my world! NO *whiskey for me,* NO NO NO*!*

And for Mattie, that weekend was confusing.

'What are you doing up so early?' Dave had asked when Mattie came into the living room at ten past five on the Saturday morning. Dave himself hadn't been able to sleep, he'd been anxious and unsettled. Mattie was barely awake.

He smiled blankly. 'I just woke up — like before, when you used to drink all night.' He was still smiling, not awake enough to realise the directness of this.

Dave frowned.

'Well, you should jump back in bed and get a few more hours sleep.'

'What's in your hand?' Mattie had spied the cup Dave was holding and, before he could answer, Mattie came over and looked into it.

'It's tea!' exclaimed Dave defensively.

'Ah, that's a pity,' replied Mattie with a yawn.

Dave was surprised. 'A pity, why?'

Mattie smiled. 'I used to like it when you were drunk.'

Dave was baffled. 'In what way?'

'It used to be so much fun — except for when you were crying …' Mattie let out a sudden giggle. 'You used to play silly games with me when you were drunk. Not like afterwards.'

Dave shook his head. He was lost, and it was easier not to face this any more. 'Go on, back up to bed.'

But Dave was unnerved. Mattie had never been so blunt in the past. When Dave thought of Mattie as a baby, he remembered their time spent together, how they'd play games and read books or simply sit and watch children's television. But as the years went on and Dave's drinking increased, his time with his son had been replaced — by arguments with June, and in nursing hangovers. A distance developed then between Mattie and Dave, with only rare moments of togetherness. Dave realised now their relationship had become almost a secret from him: unless June told him about it, the times that Mattie spent with his father early on Saturday mornings never remained in Dave's memory when he finally sobered up.

And in the same way, the hours that Dave spent at the foot of Mattie's bed watching him sleep never existed outside of that slumber. Though Mattie adored his father he'd barely known him outside of the grand conversations and fun times they shared when Dave was drunk and unworried.

Meanwhile, Dave had spent the rest of his time battling the demons in his head and watching the clock as it laboured towards the weekend once again. And where was June through all of this? She was the pillar of strength that held the family aloft, a pillar whose foundations were rapidly, secretly eroding.

Mattie had never talked back to his father and had rarely mentioned his drinking. It had been all right for June to argue with Dave about it, but it was an unspoken belief that Mattie was too young to have an opinion on such matters. Things were clearly different now, though. Dave realised that Mattie did have an opinion — and he wasn't keeping it to himself any longer.

A few days before Susan left for her father's, Mattie had said to Dave, 'So now that you're not drinking any more, do you still talk to Uncle Stephen?' Dave had been reading the newspaper and only barely caught what was said.

'What ... Uncle Stephen?'

Mattie sat up from the floor, where he'd been busy with maths homework. 'Yea — Uncle Stephen — do you still talk to him now that you're not drinking?'

Dave immediately felt defensive, and looked sharply at his son. 'Mattie, you know it's rude to ask questions like that.'

'Why?' Mattie's big blue eyes were condemning.

'Because it *is*.' Dave's voice rose.

'No, it's not!' Mattie was confident, his face perfectly passionless. For a moment Dave hardly recognised the young man sitting before him.

'Yes, it is.' Dave had frowned uneasily. 'I had a very serious illness and it's rude to talk to people about things like that, very rude.'

'So were you an alcoholic?'

Dave ran an anxious hand through his silver hair.

'An alcoholic? Where did you hear a word like that?'

'I'm nearly ten Dad, I'm not a kid.' Mattie had shaken his head indignantly but Dave wasn't having it.

'Don't shake your head like that — if you're nearly ten then you should have a bit of cop on. You don't talk to people this way and a word like *alcoholic* isn't something you just throw about.'

An awkward silence followed. Shame had pulsed between them and Mattie turned towards his homework. Unsettled, Dave breathed a heavy sigh, then continued in a calmer voice:

'Mattie, look at me for a second ...'

Mattie turned slowly.

'The truth is, I'm not really angry with you. I'm angry with myself.'

Mattie looked confused.

'I'm angry because you shouldn't have to ask me questions like that — and just so that you know, I wasn't always an alcoholic. There was a time when I could handle my drink.' Dave paused and remembered his father. 'But you're right, I became one, it got the better of me and that's why I've been going to counselling — to get some help. It won't beat me any more.' Silence followed. Mattie seemed a little unsatisfied.

'Mammy told me that you've always been an alcoholic.' Mattie had become timid.

Dave's face lit up with sudden anger. 'What?' He rose to his feet. Fury, anger, frustration, shame — a big cloud was filling him.

'She only said it once!' Mattie was upset; he never wanted to hurt his father, or harm his mother's image.

Dave crouched down, suddenly face to face with his son, and pointed his finger: 'Don't you dare!'

Mattie sat back, afraid of the growling man.

'Don't you ever use your mother against me, do you hear, don't you ever!'

Tears had welled up in Mattie's eyes. 'I'm sorry, Daddy, I was just saying what she said, I'm sorry you're angry!'

Dave rose to his feet again. 'Get back to your homework!'

Then Dave had left the room as Mattie wiped the tears from his face. He couldn't understand what he'd done wrong.

'Mattie, I'm sorry about earlier on, I didn't mean to make you cry!'

It was evening, and Dave had come to clear the air. Mattie bowed his head.

'You surprised me, that's all, I didn't expect you to talk about my drinking like that.'

Dave placed a comforting hand on Mattie's shoulder. 'Maybe I was an alcoholic all along, I don't know … your mother always seemed convinced.' Dave looked away forlornly. 'I know one thing for sure: I didn't drink all the time but when I did I found it hard to stop.'

'But you don't drink now.' Mattie spoke softly, afraid that his words might ignite another argument.

'No.' Dave smiled. 'Not any more, and I won't be talking to your uncle Stephen either. The problem with lots of alcohol is that it can make you quite emotional and stir up old memories, good and bad. You never met your uncle but he was a great man who died very young.' Dave felt a shiver as he spoke; it had been a long time since he'd talked about Stephen without the aid of a whiskey or two. 'I loved your uncle so much but before he died we had a big argument and I never had a chance to make things right.' Dave shrugged his shoulders. 'Mattie, I wish I could turn back time, there are so many things I'd do differently.'

Mattie looked blankly at Dave.

'Obviously I wouldn't change you,' he continued with a wholehearted grin. 'You're by far the best thing that has ever happened in my life.'

Mattie's face lit up and they had a warm hug.

January 1990

Mattie was late home from school again and Dave sat in the kitchen waiting for him. The hours of contemplation today, since Mattie's revelation about hitting him back in England, had seemed to go on forever.

'Where have you been? It's half past six already, school finished at four!' It wasn't how he'd planned to start their conversation; he wanted to be calm and approachable.

Mattie looked guilty. 'I was at Niall's, playing on his Commodore 64.'

Dave squashed his frustration; after all, he wanted to discuss his own wrongful actions. 'Well … it's good to have you home, I was a bit worried.'

'You don't have to worry, Dad.' Mattie tossed his schoolbag on top of the washing machine. 'I'm fine.'

'Well, your dinner's in the oven, go wash your hands and I'll heat it up for you.'

'I'm not hungry.' Mattie casually turned towards the door to the living room, where the television was humming.

'Why not?' Dave was careful not to sound impatient.

'Niall's mam made me dinner — fish fingers and chips.'

'Who's Niall?'

'My *friend*. From *school*.' Mattie threw his eyes to heaven and then disappeared through the door. Dave followed him into the living room, where he'd plonked on the couch in front of the television.

'So, how was school?'

Mattie had his feet on the couch. It was on the tip of Dave's tongue to tell him to take them off, but he let it slide this one time.

'It was okay.' Mattie didn't take his eyes from the TV screen.

'Great!' sighed Dave, trying to think of something else to say. 'And did you have any luck with your girlfriend, the one you've been gelling your hair for?'

Mattie threw an uninterested look at Dave and then returned his attention to the television.

Dave sighed again, this time louder than before, hoping that Mattie would sense he wished to have a proper conversation. But Mattie was engrossed in an evening game show. Finally, Dave rose and stood in front of the television.

'I can't see, Dad, out of the way!'

'I want to talk with you.' Dave spoke in a calm and serious tone but Mattie only shifted to try to look past his father at the screen.

'Enough of this.' Dave turned suddenly and pressed the off switch. 'Let's do without television for a few minutes.'

'Ah Dad!' Mattie whined.

'No *ah Dad*s, okay?' He remained composed. 'I need to ask you a few questions.'

Mattie folded his arms in a spoilt huff. 'What questions?'

'I need to ask you about this morning.'

'Not that again!'

'Yes, that again, I need you to tell me what happened.'

Mattie sat up uneasily in his seat. 'You never said sorry.'

'I know, I know, that's why I want to talk to you about it. I want to say sorry but I need to know what happened.'

But Mattie was reluctant. Dave tried leading him.

'I'd been drinking, right?'

'Yea.' Mattie's eyes had glazed over.

'And were we playing?' Dave smiled, trying to release his son's tongue.

'No.' Mattie turned away, annoyed. 'I don't want to talk about this any more!'

'I'm sorry, Mattie, I really don't remember — you'll have to help me.'

Reluctantly Mattie faced his father once again. Whatever warmth that had been there before had been drained. 'You were lying on the carpet.' He paused.

'Was I asleep?'

'Yea.' He turned away again. 'I walked in and tried to wake you because the floor was all wet and you were sleeping in it!'

'All wet?'

'Yea, and when I woke you up, you got a fright — you looked at the wet and then at me and then ...' Mattie stopped. He could see the dark look of shame in his father's eyes, the sudden awakening of the memory.

Dave was having an instant flashback of the entire event: the embarrassment he'd felt at being woken by his son as he slept in a stupefied heap on the floor — having just pissed himself for the second time that night. How could he have forgotten the hard slap he'd delivered to his son's face during that moment of madness and weakness and shame? Had June been there too? Had she witnessed the slap or had she entered just as the tears rolled down Mattie's face? Dave didn't know, but he remembered that hers was the face he saw immediately after his open palm made contact with Mattie's soft skin. And now he knew: it was at that exact moment that his world had come undone, in the frenzy of counteractions that had led him to the place he was right now.

June had unleashed a torrent of abuse.

'Pissed yourself again? You're nothing but the scum of the earth!' Then she'd lunged at him, hitting him roughly with her open hand and yelling out her frustration. 'You've ruined my life, you've ruined your son's life. You're an alcoholic, nothing but a pisshead! Dad was right, I should never have had anything to do with you.'

Dave remembered how drunk he was, how nothing she was saying had steadied his blurred vision and wavering attention.

'Last week I found you lying in the shower — you'd pissed yourself that time too — the things we come to!'

She continued with venom in her eyes and rage in her voice, but Dave, stumbling to his feet, was like an oil tanker that was slow to come around.

'How many times do I have to ring your boss on a Monday morning and tell him that you're sick and can't come in; he laughs at me now, he knows it's all lies!'

Dave remembered how he'd moved in on June's lips while she was ushering Mattie off to bed.

'You're trying to *kiss* me?' she yelled in disbelief as she thrust him away, his wobbling legs failing and pulling him to the ground with a slam.

'But I love you.' He was barely coherent.

'Do you know what?' June approached Dave, the flush rising in her cheeks, her tone savage. 'I was wrong all those years ago. Stephen was the better man, he's the one I should have stayed with! I wasted my life, and his, on you!'

Dave's face tightened — she'd reached him, far deeper than he could have imagined possible. With dizzy, spinning nausea he rose to his feet, the hurt flaming in his eyes.

He could hardly stand but he wasn't willing to stay in that room, its walls were closing in.

'Where are you going?' June's voice echoed his emptiness, the agonising defeat. She stepped forward to come to his rescue once again, as she'd done so many countless times in the past, but Dave had ignored her. He'd brushed by like an exhausted bull, staggering from the room.

'Come back, Dave.' Her voice was muffled by tears.

But Dave had already reached for the car keys on the bench top in the kitchen. June wouldn't be able to go after him, even though she saw what he planned to do.

As soon as the car started, it would mean the end.

Seconds later Dave was speeding up the road, towards the drink-driving test that would catch him only one kilometre from his home.

'I'm so sorry I smacked you that night.' Dave bowed his head in regret.

Mattie just gazed at him with a sorrowful smile. The vexed look had gone, but he was let down.

'I really didn't mean to, I was —' Dave couldn't say the word. He'd used it too many times with June as an excuse and he was utterly ashamed of himself. *I was drunk* carried no weight: it was like apologising for doing something you'd had no control over, when the reality was quite the opposite. And now that the memory had returned, he knew he'd see that night in his head time and time again.

'I'm really sorry, son, it'll never happen again. I *promise* you, as long as I live, it'll never happen again.'

Mattie's smile grew. 'It's okay, Daddy, it didn't really hurt!'

Dave winced.

'Can we watch the television again?'

Some noise, some activity was needed.

'Of course, of course we can.'

Dave switched on the television. The game show host was still prancing about on the screen in his blue pin-striped suit and exaggerated moustache. Mattie's eyes moved firmly to the screen, but Dave could see the distance in his gaze. There was no scar on his son's face, no mark where he'd hit him — but the impression that was left in the boy's mind would remain: Dave knew he would never be able to remove it.

March 1990

Dave gazed at the blisters of paint that hung like stalactites from the bedroom ceiling. Even from something as inconsequential as peeling paint, memories found a way of surfacing.

'I should have let you do the painting, I never had the patience,' Dave whispered to the stillness of the room, picturing June with the paint roller in her hand, and her wide, strong grin. They'd had so much enjoyment making their house a home. June had preferred painting, and Dave did all the handy work. He'd spent days building shelves and knocking in nails while June brought colour to the walls. The ceiling of their bedroom came last.

'Let me do it,' insisted Dave. 'You look tired, I'll finish it off for you.'

'Are you sure?' She was exhausted and strain pulled at her shoulders.

'You go have a bath and when you come back, naked,' Dave smiled suggestively, 'I'll be ready for you.'

June swanned past Dave with a cheeky grin and a kiss — and a swift dab of the roller to his chin. Her laughter echoed in the room. Then the bathroom door shut and water began to fill the tub. Dave loved seeing June like that; it always convinced him that he was doing the right thing, for a change.

It was only a few years later, really, and the ceiling dripped broken paint. If I wasn't so damn horny that night, I wouldn't have rushed the paint job as much. He smiled and turned his head towards the empty space in bed beside him.

'I'd give anything to see you lying there, June, anything,' he sighed. She always wore perfume, a sweet fragrance that would linger on her pillow, even when she wasn't around. That aroma was no longer there and, looking at their bedroom, Dave felt as though the life they once had was all but gone. Had even the past given up on him?

The old, round-faced clock ticked on the bedside table. Ten past four in the morning. Dave couldn't relax. He thought about Mattie, and about his own life to date. He thought about the drunkenness and the gap it had caused between them. He thought about Stephen and about England, but most of all he thought about his wife. The slender grace with which she always held herself. Her voice, echoing in his head. June always seemed to have an answer for everything, a wise solution to a problem, a kind suggestion to ease a troubled mind.

'You'd know what to do now, June,' he exclaimed. 'If you were lying here beside me you'd be able to tell me exactly how to deal with Mattie.'

As Susan had promised, her father's plans had not materialised. This was a relief for Dave, as he couldn't face such a conflict. But today had been a terrible day.

It began quite simply. Dave had prepared breakfast, during which he and Mattie came to be speaking about June.

'When were you talking to her?'

'She walked me to school yesterday.'

'Did she?' Dave could hardly contain himself. 'And did she say anything about me?'

Mattie had regarded his father coolly and shook his head. 'No, why would she?' Mattie began to play with his breakfast, no longer interested in it.

'She didn't say anything at all?'

'No, Dad, stop asking me.'

Dave looked away, unsatisfied with this but resigned, for now. Then Mattie had dropped his spoon on the floor.

'Are you not hungry, do you not like your porridge?'

'I don't like your food.' Mattie's tone was respectful enough but his words were clearly insulting. The abruptness of it had shocked Dave so much that he'd simply cowered down behind his mug of coffee.

But tonight, having mulled it over at work for most of the day, Dave had thought it best to discuss it.

'This morning at breakfast, Mattie, you seemed annoyed with me.'

Mattie offered his father a false smile. 'No, I just hate your food.'

Dave's lips tightened. 'That's not a very nice thing to say to someone. I didn't see you offering to make breakfast.'

'That's your job, not mine. Anyway, it's the truth, your food stinks!'

'Stinks?' Dave was angry, but he remained composed.

'Yea, it *stinks*,' shouted Mattie, his mouth pursing with distaste. Suddenly he leapt up and ran to put on his shoes.

'Where are you going? We're having a discussion here,' Dave said, following him.

'No, we're not. I'm going out to play football!' Mattie was defiant, and Dave could no longer hold back his anger.

'No, you are not.' Dave put a firm hand on Mattie's arm, restraining him.

'Are you going to hit me again?' Mattie's eyes had narrowed and the words landed straight to Dave's heart.

He immediately released his hold on the boy, and Mattie dashed for the back door. Dave was weakened, stripped. As Mattie bounced a ball on the concrete surface of the backyard, Dave collapsed in a desperate heap on the living room couch.

What's going on here? he thought. What am I doing wrong? There had been other remarks from Mattie — but none so hurtful, none cast with such spite. Saying no to turning off the television or brushing your teeth was hardly major and Dave had overlooked these small rebellions, even though his son had never been so bold in the past. But *this*, the food and then using the events of England as ammunition — well, it was totally out of order. Dave gritted his teeth and stood up.

'I'm damned if I'm standing for it!'

Gathering his sense of paternal authority, Dave followed Mattie into the backyard. The boy was kicking his soccer ball against the shed wall. Each powerful smack against the red brick seemed to mimic Dave's heartbeat as he approached. He reached Mattie at the exact moment his foot made striking contact against the ball. Mattie leapt, startled, when Dave tapped his shoulder.

'Get your hands off me,' he yelled, spinning around and backing away.

'Mattie.' Dave was in control, his stern influence renewed. 'Don't you dare talk to me like that. I'm your father and you will obey me.' He didn't shout, but spoke strongly — more strongly then he usually would so close to the other houses.

Mattie's face was flushed. 'You can't tell me what to do, you have no say over me.' Mattie stepped further away, until his back was against the shed wall and there was nowhere else for him to go. 'Get away from me! Get your hands off of me — somebody call the police!'

Dave looked at his son with horror. He had no hold on Mattie, he was barely within reach of him! What was going on?

From the house next door Dave could hear the sound of footsteps as Mattie went on yelling — this left Dave with no choice but to reach out and take hold of his son.

'Mattie! Stop it! *Stop* this, now.'

'He's hitting me, call the police, he's hurting me!'

'*Mattie*,' Dave's voice rose desperately, 'have you gone mad or something? Stop this, please, son, for God's sake stop this —' With a swift pull, Dave dragged his son into a tight embrace. Mattie didn't let up, battling ferociously against the firm hold, tugging this way and that, but getting nowhere. Dave wasn't going to give in, he couldn't.

'Is everything all right in there, Dave?'

Her voice startled them both. It was Shelley from next door.

Mattie stood still at last, and Dave felt a wash of embarrassment.

'It's all fine, Shelley.' He kept his back to her. 'Mattie isn't himself today.'

'Is that right?' Her voice sounded closer and Dave turned stiffly.

Shelley's jowly, keen-eyed face was peering at him over the wall. Dave immediately let go of his son, who was suddenly the exemplar of innocence.

'Shelley ...' He heard guilt in his voice. 'How long have you been standing there?'

'Long enough, Dave!' With remote distaste, she studied both of them.

Dave felt like he needed to defend himself, but was too mortified to try.

'Are you all right, Mattie?' quizzed Shelley in a disciplinary-like manner, her sharp eyes fixed on the young man.

'Yea,' nodded Mattie.

'Well, you're lucky! If you were my son I would have reddened your arse with a wooden spoon for the way that you were behaving!'

Relief filled Dave's face, and he nodded in acknowledgement. 'Aye, you're right, Shelley, I've never seen him as bold.'

Mattie looked like a wounded lion, brought down in his tracks.

'Shouting like that at your father, you should be ashamed of yourself!' Shelley continued, her pale cheeks reddening as she spoke. 'I never once heard you talk to your mother like that! Have you no respect, no manners?'

Dave glanced at Mattie, his youthfulness drained and replaced by worry and shame. Suddenly Dave couldn't bear to see him like that.

'That's enough, Shelley,' he interrupted. She was surprised, and then regret flashed across her face.

'Oh —' she said. 'Of course, sorry, I got a bit carried away there.'

'You're all right, Shelley,' he reassured, 'I'll take it from here.'

'Absolutely!' Shelley's round head disappeared, and they heard her back door close. Dave turned to Mattie.

'Are you okay?'

'Sorry, Dad!' His voice came from Dave's chest, where he'd buried his head.

Dave was still confused. 'What's come over you lately, Mattie, have you listened to yourself?'

'Sorry, Daddy.' Mattie looked up, his eyes big with regret.

'I don't want to hear you talking back to me again … What would your mam say?' Dave hesitated. But then, thinking of how June would feel if she'd seen this, he continued, 'Will you be telling her about how rude you were?'

Mattie bowed his head once again. 'No.'

'Well, you should, maybe she can talk some sense into you.'

Silence followed. A cool breeze skipped across the yard, settling a chill on everything it touched.

'Can I go?' Mattie had had enough.

So had Dave. 'Go on.'

Dave watched as his son scampered into the house. A few minutes earlier, he'd barely resembled a boy: the anger had stolen his bright youth. And something still wasn't right with him.

But Dave felt the will and the strength had been sapped from him, and all that came to mind was whiskey.

As night came on, there was also a dense fog of tension inside the house, an air of confusion and hurt. Father and son sat on the couch, gazing at the television, neither saying a word. Finally it was Mattie's bedtime, and the usual nightly pleasantries had to take place.

'It's time for bed, Mattie.'

Mattie didn't react.

'Mattie,' Dave repeated in a sterner tone, 'it's time for bed.'

'I don't want to go.' He spoke softly, distantly.

'Is everything all right?'

'I can't sleep.'

Dave sat forward, giving Mattie his full attention, though the boy still stared at the television. 'You can't sleep? Why, are you worried about something? Are you frightened?'

'I'm not frightened,' declared Mattie now, turning to glance at his father, 'I just can't sleep.'

Dave pondered. 'You must be thinking about something. What's going through your head?'

Mattie bit his lip and Dave saw his uneasiness.

'It's okay, you can tell me. Is it something that I've done?'

Mattie looked at his father and shook his head, 'No.' He looked away again.

'Is it because you and I have been …' Dave spoke cautiously '… fighting a bit lately?' Silence followed. 'Because, you know, it's pretty normal for a father and son to have problems from time to time — believe me, I didn't always see eye to eye with my dad.'

Mattie shifted in his seat, tuning in.

'Everybody argues and there's no reason why we should be any different.' Dave paused. 'It's not very nice, I know, but sometimes it has to happen so that we understand each other better.'

Mattie looked at his father with confusion. 'Understand?'

'Yes, we learn to understand one another. You're your own person, you have some of my personality traits and some of your mother's but altogether you've got your own personality. It's hard for people to always agree, but the one thing I would say is that when I get angry with you for back-talking or misbehaving, it's only because I want the best for you. I want you to grow up and be the best you can be and it's my job to do everything in my power to make that happen, even if it means telling you off from time to time.'

Mattie smiled softly, which pleased Dave.

'That's the spirit,' exclaimed Dave, putting a gentle arm around Mattie's shoulders. 'I haven't seen you smile in days ...'

But no sooner had Mattie's smile arrived than it disappeared again, as though a chip had been taken from his heart.

'What's wrong?' Dave was baffled. 'Where's my smile gone to, I love it when you smile, you make me think of your mother.'

Mattie flinched. 'Stop talking about Mammy!' There was the anger again.

'What?' Dave faced his son.

'I'm sick of you talking about Mammy — *that's* why I can't sleep.'

'You can't sleep because I mention your mam — what's that supposed to mean?'

Mattie's eyes burned with disappointment. 'Why don't you just get back together? You keep talking about her and making me angry — I want you to get back together with her!'

Dave was perplexed. 'But, Mattie,' he sighed, 'I can't get back together with her. If I could —'

'*Why* can't you? Why?' Mattie rose to his feet. 'Do you not love her?'

'Of course I love her. I love her more than anything in this world.'

'Then get back together with her!' Mattie yelled the words and Dave closed his eyes, guilt and frustration running through his veins. He desperately wanted a drink.

'Mattie,' he spoke slowly and with deep sincerity, 'I can't, I wish I could, but it's not how things are meant be.'

Mattie stepped back. 'See, it's your fault, everything is your fault —' He was suddenly furious, pointing at his father like a hunter with a rifle. 'If you didn't drink, none of this would have happened, Mammy would still be in the house and everyone would be happy. No one would be making fun of me at school!'

'Making fun of you?'

'They all think there's something wrong with me, everybody makes fun of me and the girls said they hated my hair. Everything's just different and it's all your fault.'

Dave allowed a moment for Mattie to calm down. Then he spoke quietly. 'Mattie … why didn't you tell me that people were making fun of you at school?'

'Because it doesn't matter. Who cares?'

'I care, that's who. Haven't I always done my best to look out for you? I can sort this out too.'

'No, you can't, not unless you and Mammy get back together!'

Dave took a moment to think. 'Mattie, I know what all my drinking has done and I'm sorry more than you'll ever understand, but you know that's not why your mammy and I aren't together —'

'Dave.' Susan stood at the doorway, her arms folded, grimly impatient.

Dave jumped. 'I didn't hear you — didn't even know you were coming.' There was a tremble in his voice.

'Mattie, you run off to bed, I need to chat with your daddy for a while.' Susan wasn't usually firm, so she'd caught Mattie by surprise. She went to him with a quick hug. 'I don't want to hear a word about it, off to bed.'

Mattie didn't say goodnight to either of them. He turned on his heel and left the room, then stamped heavily up the staircase and into his bedroom.

'What are you doing?' Susan couldn't contain her frustration. 'I warned you when I left to stop talking about her — didn't I tell you it wouldn't do either of you any good? But what are you still doing?'

'What *can* I do, Susan?' He sounded desperate. 'I miss her like crazy. I'm falling to pieces here — and I need a drink so fucking badly it's ridiculous!' Dave dropped his head and stared at the floor.

'I don't care, Dave.' Susan's voice rose. 'If you want sympathy you're talking to the wrong person. God knows you've had a lifetime to solve your drinking problems, it's your tough luck that you're finally doing it now.' She regathered her thoughts. 'I don't want to talk about you and your addiction, the only person I'm concerned about is Mattie. Was I wrong to respect your private time with him and wait so long before visiting? How often do you talk to Mattie about June?'

Dave faced Susan. 'Every day.'

'Every day!' She was astonished. 'Are you insane?'

'But he speaks to her all the time. You know that. When she walks him to school, even Terry chats with her. I don't see what the problem is.'

Susan was horrified. 'Dave, are you hearing what you're saying? You're sitting there, telling me that your son is talking to June every day when you know she isn't here, do you know how that sounds?' Susan bit her lip, closing her eyes briefly, trying to contain the tears. She ran her hand across her forehead.

'Don't cry, Susan, please don't cry.'

'How can I not?' She began to sniffle. 'Mattie has almost no friends at school any more, he gets mocked every day, they all say the poor kid is nuts. Terry is nothing but an old fool who thinks he's being nice to Mattie — he's doing more harm than good, just like you are.' Tears coursed down her cheeks.

'That's not true, Susan, that is not true.' He stood in front of her.

'And what about me? How do you think it makes me feel, hearing you talking like this? Do you not realise that it's not just you who is falling to pieces, I am, we all are!'

Her eyes met Dave's. He rested a comforting hand on her head, and they held each other until her sobbing finally subsided.

'Dave,' she pulled back from him, 'why do you do this to Mattie?'

Dave stepped uncomfortably away.

'*Dave*,' she yelled, 'why are you doing this to your only son? To me? Why are you doing this to yourself?'

Dave turned his back on Susan.

'Answer me!' There was fury in her voice as she tugged him roughly by the shoulders, forcing him to face her. 'Why are you doing this? Why do you keep talking to your son as though nothing has happened? She's dead, Dave!'

Susan drew Dave's face close to her own. 'June is dead, Dave. We buried her in the family grave at my mother's house, she's *dead*.'

Susan let go of him as the sobs racked her body.

Dave stood motionless, his face expressionless. Slowly he turned to look at Susan, who was battling with the reality of what she'd said.

'Because at least he gets to talk to her.' Dave spoke softly, almost in a whisper.

'What?' Susan looked up, wiping her cheeks.

'I ask Mattie about her because at least he gets to talk to her. I've got nothing.' Dave pressed his eyes. 'When I close my eyes now and try to imagine her, I can hardly see her face any more. It's like I'm losing her for a second time.' Dave couldn't hold back any longer, he fell to his knees and began to cry softly.

'I loved her, Susan, I loved her so much. And now she's gone. She's gone from this world, gone from my mind, I'll never see her again.'

Susan cradled him in her arms, saying nothing, giving him time to face his pain.

'Why didn't *I* die, I've been nothing but a fuck-up all my life! Why would God take away an angel and leave someone like me behind instead?'

'Don't talk like that, Dave.'

'It's true.'

Susan said no more, there was nothing left to say.

'I just miss her so much, Susan, what will I do without her?'

'You'll become the man that she always knew you could be.'

'And what about Mattie?'

'You'll have to look after him. He needs to come to terms with this.'

'But why does he talk to her like he does, what's wrong with him?'

'I don't know, Dave.' Her gaze drifted. 'It all started after the funeral … He wouldn't come to it, and he locked himself in his room for days. When he finally came out he seemed fine, but a few days later he started mentioning things — things about June. I didn't have the heart to stop him — I think, just like you, a part of me wanted to believe that somehow she was still here. But she wasn't, she isn't. You need to straighten him out.'

'I don't think I've got the strength.'

'Well then you need to find it! When you returned from England I told you that June had died, and instead of being there for us all, you ran away and drank yourself nearly to death. Now you're back.' She paused. 'And it's time you made June proud!'

June 1989

'Home sweet home, home sweet home ...'

June was repeating the phrase continuously, slurring her words and stuttering. Susan glanced quickly at her again.

'Oh Jesus Christ!' She had slammed on the brakes so hard that Mattie was jerked from his sleep in the back seat of the car.

'What's wrong?' he cried. 'What's happened to Mammy?'

'Home sweet home! Home sweet home!' June's head was swaying. Car horns sounded as Susan pulled over. She leapt out and ran round to drag June from the car and onto the road. Cars on both sides of the motorway slowed down to take a look at what was happening — then other drivers were rushing to Susan and Mattie's aid.

June was still speaking but her eyes were dilated and she was shaking horribly, as though overcome by a sudden chill. Susan had rested her on her back, propping her head up on a cardigan from the back seat.

'Does she have epilepsy?' one motorist asked calmly.

'No,' replied Susan, who was now trying to soothe Mattie.

'We need to get her to hospital,' the man said. 'Right now.'

Someone sped off for help and after a time an ambulance came. June was lying in a heap in her sister's arms, and Mattie was crying beside her. The sounding of horns had stopped, and cars banked up quietly around them.

Susan tried to guard Mattie from the sight of his mother; the usual lustre and resilience of her face had been lost, and with a respiratory mask over her mouth she looked lifeless. But Mattie resisted. He gazed at his mother.

June had a strong heartbeat when they arrived at the hospital, but it was almost six hours before a doctor finally met Susan and Mattie in the waiting area.

The doctor took her to a quiet room, leaving Mattie to wait, and then Susan knew that it was bad news.

'What's happened?' Susan felt frantic but, beneath that, something told her that the situation was out of her hands now.

The doctor drew breath and looked steadily at Susan. 'She suffered what's called a intracerebral brain haemorrhage, or bleeding into the brain tissue.'

Susan felt a stab to her chest and began to breathe heavily.

'I'm so sorry, I really am.' The doctor's eyes were warm and filled with sincere sympathy. 'She's on life support now,' he continued with care, 'but all of her bodily functions are shutting down ... she doesn't have long.'

Susan felt faint, her legs became weak and she could hardly stand.

'Come over here.' The doctor put his arm around her and led her to a seat. 'Let me get you some water.'

Susan felt a tremor in her hands and a sickness in her stomach. Her life with June flooded through her mind as though she were the one facing death. She took deep gasps of air and tried to sip the water. She remembered her older sister playing with her in primary school when Susan felt frightened to be away from her mother. She remembered the endless arguments about whose turn it was to do the washing-up after dinner and about how long somebody could stand in front of the vanity mirror in the bathroom. She remembered the secrets they shared, the games they played and, most passionately, the love they had for one another, which had grown stronger as they matured. She remembered Christmas times and mince pies which June devoured and Susan hated and for a brief second she saw June's brilliant smile beaming into her eyes.

'You should go and see her now,' urged the doctor, 'and if you give the names and numbers of other family members to the nurse, she'll see that they're all informed.'

Susan had a moment of terrible clarity. 'Dave, he's her husband. He's in England!'

'Do you know his number?' The doctor spoke softly.

'No —' Susan became distressed. 'I have it written down at home somewhere. Is there … time … to get him here? Should I — '

'She has, I'm sorry, only hours. Concentrate on her and the boy. If you remember anything about the husband's address, let us know.'

A radio hummed in the background but did little to muffle the sounds of beeping instruments and grinding ventilators. In the six hours that had passed since the ambulance journey, June had already changed; it was as though someone had taken her place. She was propped up in the hospital bed but her eyes were shut and Susan knew that she was no longer there.

'She has the heart of a lion,' comforted the doctor. 'She's not willing to let go.'

'She's probably holding on for Dave,' Susan whispered.

Mattie was still back in the waiting room, being looked after by a friendly old nurse with a loud laugh.

'What will I do about her son?' Susan asked the doctor as she wept, holding June's soft hand in hers.

'Bring him in, it's important that he says goodbye.'

'But he's only nine!' Susan cried. 'He's only a boy …'

The doctor nodded. 'I know, but still, he should see her before she's gone.'

The doctor touched her shoulder then left the room. Susan was alone with her sister.

'June,' she sobbed, 'why has this happened to you? I don't understand.'

Susan knew that it wouldn't be long before her mam and dad would arrive and hysterics would take over everything that was unfolding. She didn't have long.

She rested her head on the bed. 'I need you, June, we all do. Don't go!' Susan sat up, peering at her sister, hoping that her eyes would suddenly open — and then realising that they wouldn't.

'I love you, June,' she breathed desperately, 'I don't want to lose you! Please, God, don't take my sister, please don't.'

When Susan finally collected Mattie, her face was suddenly much older — the tears and the pain that she tried hard to conceal had marked her skin.

'What's wrong, Aunty Susan?'

Susan clenched her teeth and battled back the grief. 'Your mammy's very sick, Mattie.' She struggled to speak, and took Mattie into her embrace. 'She's very sick, Mattie, and you need to come and see her now.' But there wasn't time.

When they got to June's room, nurses were rushing around, hurriedly tending to her while a continuous sound blurted from the heart monitor. The radio still played a lonely song that ripped through Susan's heart.

Is there anyone out there, are their faces beyond
   the dark
The light that we used to know, is like the tears
   I cannot show in this place here all alone
Years wondering what to do, spent so much of it
   doing nothing

And now lying here on my back, I'd trade this
  space for just one second of the world I could
  have known
And so, what's the use in crying out, if
  someone's waiting on the outside, hoping for
  a sign, then you could
Stay, don't go away.
Stay, don't go away.

What happened to yesterday, all the simple
  things seemed to lose their way
Now I wonder what I forgot, like the words I
  should have said to the ones who'd seen it all
And so, what's the use in crying out, if
  someone's waiting on the outside, hoping for
  a sign, then you could
Stay, don't go away.
Stay, don't go away.

Susan turned abruptly. She couldn't allow Mattie to see what was happening — he *couldn't* witness the doctors' and nurses' futile attempts to help June. He was too young, it was too much for a child to bear.

Taking his hand, Susan led Mattie out of view.

A boy shouldn't have that sort of memory of his mother, thought Susan, he should only remember her as beautiful and healthy and alive.

March 1990

A flake of paint fell from the ceiling. The time on the round clock was now almost six. Dave hadn't slept all night — he couldn't. After his talk yesterday with Susan, he was left feeling empty and utterly alone. June was dead and denial wasn't going to bring her back.

'*Now that the day has taken you away.*' A song circled in his mind. '*I pray that someone will tell me things will be okay, but I want you to know, you're always on my mind.*' He sat up in his bed, 'And I'll wait for you, for all of time.' The last words he sang aloud and in a small way it managed to raise his spirits, rousing him to his feet. He scanned the room in all directions and then he smiled. 'We did our best, June,' he spoke with reverence. 'It wasn't perfect, but it wasn't all bad either — now it's time to move on.' Dave kissed the palm of his hand then pressed it against the cold wall, resting it there for a moment. 'I love you, baby!' He left the room and immediately entered Mattie's.

'Mattie,' Dave whispered at the foot of the sleeping boy's bed, 'Mattie, time to wake up!'

Mattie didn't respond so Dave moved closer. 'Mattie,' he prodded the youngster's shoulder, 'Mattie, we have to go.'

'Where ...' He yawned, his eyes still half closed, 'Where are we going?'

'We're going to Mayo, to visit your mother.'

Mattie's eyes opened wide. 'Mayo? But we don't need to drive all the way up there.' Mattie seemed suddenly wary. 'We can see her here, we can all walk to school together!'

Dave looked at his son. He breathed as though he was about to swim a kilometre underwater. Mattie tried to escape his gaze but he took the boy's face in gentle hands. 'You know the truth, Mattie. Just like I do. We can't pretend any more — it's no good. You know your mam has died, Mattie, don't you? We have to say goodbye.'

Mattie bit his lip. 'But we can see her here, we can see her ...' Mattie suddenly turned away from Dave. 'We can see her here.'

Dave knew that Mattie was trying to disguise the onset of tears. 'Come here, son.' Mattie didn't respond so Dave reached out and grabbed his son in a strong embrace.

The little boy shuddered and a shout escaped him. 'Mammy! I want my mam! I want her *back*.' He sobbed and struggled and Dave held him fast.

'I love you, do you know that, I love you so much.'

Mattie burrowed into his chest and the real tears came for both of them. 'You're all I have in this world now,' whispered Dave as he held him tightly, 'I'll always protect you.'

'You guys are up early!' commented Susan, who'd stayed the night and was awake in the living room when father and son entered.

'There's something that we have to do.'

Susan could see that Mattie had been crying and her heart sank; but he came to her and wrapped his arms around her waist.

Dave approached her and kissed her on the forehead. 'We're going to do what we should have done a long time ago.' He took a deep breath. 'We're going to go for a drive today to Mayo and we'll say goodbye to the love of our lives.' He smiled gently. 'We'll remember June.'

Acknowledgments

Many thanks to Judith Lukin-Amundsen, Linda Funnell, Kate O'Donnell, Anna Valdinger, Gaye Kalnins and Jennifer Fontaine for their assistance with this project.

From the book to the album,
discover the songs that are a part of
Remember June

DAMIENLEITH
REMEMBER JUNE

REMEMBER JUNE CD AVAILABLE NOW

"…touches of Keane's beefy piano-led pop/rock, plus some Muse-style dramatic guitar, while still keeping Leith's trademark harmonies and sky high vocals, a bigger-sounding album"

"It's clear Remember June is a stand out album. It's also a wake up call for the music industry to take Leith more seriously. [Remember June] lifts Leith's original music to a new level. There is a notable absence of cover songs and crooning, with an emphasis on pop rock with an edge. Better still, it's enjoyable in its entirety, with strong tracks from start to finish"

"Forget what you knew about former Australian Idol Damien Leith and start here. His musicianship is stronger than ever and his band is rocking. Lead single 'To Get To You' is an impressive platform to kick off from"

"You can hear the stadium anthem hallmarks of U2, Coldplay and Snow Patrol… [Remember June] borrows from the 'oh-way-oh' crowd-pleasing rock-camp of bands mentioned above, stirs in his Celtic folk roots and follows the concept of two lovers fighting the inevitable end of their union"

WWW.DAMIENLEITH.COM.AU | WWW.BANDIT.FM/DAMIENLEITH | WWW.FACEBOOK.COM/DAMIENLEITH

Follow Damien on twitter @DamienLeith

A trek through Nepal ...
A confronting obsession ...

Damien
LEITH

One More Time

A NOVEL

One more step ...
One more secret ...
One more time.

Sean is in Nepal on a trek through some of the most beautiful — and dangerous — country in the world. His path takes him to the spectacular Annapurna Mountains, and deep into territory filled with Maoist guerrillas challenging the Nepalese government. Yet the local people are friendly, the air is clear, and it's easy to become accustomed to the national dish of *dal bhat*.

With each step, however, Sean's thoughts turn towards home and his family in Dublin, and it becomes clear that the obstacles he faces are greater than guerrillas demanding 'donations' or the reckless behaviour of fellow travellers.

Why did he leave Ireland so hurriedly? What makes people regard him so strangely? And what about the beautiful Serena, last seen on an idyllic beach in India, who has inspired him to take this journey? As Sean travels through Nepal, events run out of his control.

If he is to survive he must find the courage to let his secret go.

9 780732 286828